MW01094230

Prelude to a
riot

prelude to a riot

to a

riot

a novel

annie
zaidi

ALEPH

ALEPH BOOK COMPANY
An independent publishing firm
promoted by *Rupa Publications India*

First published in India in 2019
by Aleph Book Company
7/16 Ansari Road, Daryaganj
New Delhi 110 002

ISBN: 978-93-88292-81-8

1 3 5 7 9 10 8 6 4 2

For sale in the Indian subcontinent only.

Printed at Replika Press Pvt. Ltd, Sonepat.

For my eklauta brother, who is also laakhon mein ek,
Aman. He is what the world needs more of.

People

Appa—Owner of a midsize estate

Devaki—Appa's daughter

Vinny—Appa's son and heir

Bavna—Vinny's wife and mother to two teenage daughters

Saju—Devaki's husband and Abu's friend

Garuda—Social Science teacher at the local high school

Kadir—Owner of Royal Bakery, the oldest in town

Mariam—Cook in Dada's household, works as a masseuse on the side

Dada—Owner of a midsize estate

Abu—Dada's grandson

Fareeda—Dada's granddaughter

Yashika—Fareeda's classmate and best friend

Deepika—Fareeda's classmate

Mommad—Migrant labourer

Majju—Mommad's nephew

Garuda Wades through Medieval History with Class 10-B

A man, once his bum is firmly attached to a big chair, modifies his name suitably. He needs a name of cosmic significance. Light of the World. Moon-Glory Hovering over the World. Lord of the Skies. The Terrible. Divine Flame. Ocean Pearl. The Universe Itself.

Problem with this guy was, he wasn't very fancy. He sounded like just another brown guy. Maybe he felt that way, too. His father was an ordinary soldier, one of those who worked their way up. Slave dynasty type.

No, no. Not an actual slave. He soldiered up the ranks. A common man, sort of. Many new dynasties were formed in this way. Even kings have to trust someone, right? And they do not trust their own family members for obvious reasons. If you remember your ancient history, Ajatshatru-Bimbisara. Recall?

Ah! Bad question, Garuda. Never ask 10-B if they recall what we did last semester.

Onwards! This guy, Hyder, was a solid fighter. Heart like a tiger. Brain also superb. How do we know? Well, if he wasn't smarter and more useful—see, finally it comes down to being useful to the king, and he was very useful. Why else was he hired? Why was he promoted? Just for fun? See, the establishment always needs a few upstart generals. But eventually, the fellow gets wise. He starts to think, aha! The king cannot do without me. This means, it is I who deserve to be king. So he makes himself equal in power to the king. Then his son inherits his power.

He never went to school, you know? Couldn't read. But he had his fierce heart and his soldier's smarts. There was serious fighting in those days. Not like nowadays. Flying above, bombing the whole country. Civilians, women, children, dogs, cats, caterpillars. In fact, there's no need to even fly overhead these days. You just push one button and a missile does the job. Who needs courage these days to go to war?

They're upping your fees next year. Did you know? Air-conditioned classrooms. So you all don't have to rot in this heat. What they'll to do about power cuts, I don't

2

know. Your school is going International. Have you heard? Capital I, International.

They will probably need two white faces to put on the faculty list. Otherwise nobody takes 'International' seriously. Your parents will want to see a white face if they are going to pay that kind of fat fees. Black faces will not do. Botswana does not qualify as international. Chinese faces are risky. Your parents can't tell Nepal from China. Nor can I. Border-nation peoples. You can't tell Nepalese from Chinese just by looking at a face. At any rate, I would be happier if they hired Nepalese teachers rather than Americans or Japanese.

Do you know how certain kinds of rot affect fruit? From the outside, the fruit looks fine. You start eating. You don't feel the rot until there's a gravelly bitterness on your tongue. That's the thing. The white man has left us to rot from the inside out.

These are instruments of confinement. Bench, desk, blackboard, cane. They taught us to sit like one teaches a dog. Put up a paw, shake hands, nice doggy. Sit, stay! Don't change your desk every day. The white man disliked confusion. Brown people, we are more complicated. We don't mind chaos. Crowds and noise. Not just on festival days. We thrive on chaos. No traffic rules. Cows, donkeys, monkeys. Everything is tolerated. What we do not tolerate is movement. Social mobility.

Prelude to a Riot

Do you understand the difference? Movement is not a byproduct of confusion. And it is not temporary. It is seeking new positions, maybe permanent positions. Movement versus inertia. Static versus kinetic? You must have read all this in Physics.

To give you an example, take your people, Fareeda. They might have been something else before they converted.

Yes, okay. Maybe you did come all the way from Arabia on a ship. Who knows? But even in Arabia, before the seventh century, people did convert. Here comes a new religion, a new messiah. People liked what they heard, or sensed that the winds of power were blowing in a new direction. They changed their identity so that the wind would be behind them, filling their sails. They travelled, and the same thing happened all over the world. One thousand years ago, or four hundred years ago. Kings won battles, sure. You know the word 'zeal'?

Where is your pocket dictionary? No, everyone does not need to look it up. Deepika, please look up zeal: z-e-a-l. Read it out for the class.

Now the thing is, even though people might bow to the zeal of a new king, they do not easily revert to their old identity once that ruler dies, or is deposed. Why?

Is it because people have discovered that there is something of value in the new faith? Or is it that they no longer need to crawl for the crumbs of approval from the old establishment? Or maybe, they discover that it's all the same, this identity or that.

Anyway. Point is, elites dislike movement. White elites are thrown out of the country, yet everyone is still sitting in their assigned caste places. Some of you, you have hundreds of acres of land. Your ancestors were rewarded with land. Pampered by generations of kings, brown as well as white. Even those who couldn't keep their backsides attached to the throne without the help of mercenary soldiers, they doled out land as a reward, and they took it away as punishment. You think you inherited your land because of your talents? How many of you would pass a farming test?

The bell will ring in ten minutes. No need to look at your watch, Yashika. That's the third time you've looked at it.

What I am saying is, you must learn to weave bamboo. Hand-fans made of bamboo. Electric fans, air conditioners, generators are all fine but twenty-four-hour power supply is not possible. Not for all. Most of you, sixty per cent of this class will get only two hours' of power supply every day. Give it ten years.

You don't believe me? You want me to write it down and sign a piece of paper? I can do that. Come back and talk to Garuda sir in ten years.

They will start by rationing diesel. Electricity will become very expensive. You will get married and have three kids each. Stop giggling. You will struggle to find clean water. Have you heard of climate change imperialism?

We'll discuss it in Geography. For now we must read History. After the school goes International, you will have different teachers for Geography, History and Civics. They will not call it 'Civics' then. They will call it Anthropology and Political Science. But as of now, they expect you to be civic rather than political.

If only we had had the sense to unite behind a strong, brown ruler three hundred years ago, we could have reversed the imperial onslaught. He would have kept our wealth here. He would have built better weapons. He would not send brown soldiers to fight for the freedom of white people across the seven seas. Tiger heart, yes, but he also had a brain.

Open your books to page 147. Fareeda! Please read out the first two paragraphs.

Annie Zaidi

Fareeda's Soliloquy

Dada must be losing his eyesight or else he'd have seen it's pointless. The way he goes on breaking his back over that runt of a tree that won't give us the littlest banana. He keeps saying it will. *Wait and see. It will. This year.*

This year, that year, next year. Next year, my brother says, it will no longer matter. Banana, pepper, the estate, none of it. Our grandfather, he says, must be the only person in town who does not see it coming. I asked him, what's coming?

You are such a baby, and you are stuck here. But our grandfather is not a baby. He is stuck here on purpose. He travels around, he knows people. He should be able to see it coming.

When I returned from school, I thought of asking our grandfather about this 'it' that's supposed to be coming. I found him in the garden, bent over and whispering to that same stupid banana plant. Then he saw me and made a loud sniffling sound near a flower. Pretending to have a cold. As if I don't know he talks to the plants.

I asked him straight off. Do you see it coming?

Patience. Love and patience. Nothing it can't do. A lily will bloom in the desert. What did they tell us about the land? When my father, your great-grandfather came here, they said nothing would ever grow here. For fifty thousand rupees, they were glad to get rid of it. Now see!

But they never loved the land. When you love, you don't just scratch the surface. You dig deep, gently uncover. Listen to what the earth is trying to say. What is her need? See what's under her skin. Too much rock? Loosen it, break it, give it your marrow. First, you sacrifice in love—

I stamped my foot hard as if to shake off an ant crawling up my socks. Mariam has told me a hundred times not to do this in front of Dada. It is rude, she says. *You are not two years old.*

That's her favourite theme. Me not being two years old. I make it a point to stamp several times. That way, I am not stamping my foot like a kid. More like, I'm trying to kill some ant or centipede. But Dada knows. At once he stopped talking about love. I tried again.

What's this thing that's coming? How come my brother and everyone else in town can see 'it'?

The straps of my schoolbag were digging into my shoulders. His fingers, tipped with crescents of dirt, rubbed the waxy leaves, hovered over the pinched petals of a flower. Then he started to poke the banana stem all over, like Doctor Aunty used to poke my stomach when it hurt.

What makes you ask, little baby? Do you see anything coming?

I scuffed my shoes in the mud. The tiffin thing with Yashika and Deepika. I hadn't said a word last week. If I told him now, he would ask, why didn't you tell me before? He may insist on going to the school to have a word with the principal.

I shook my head. I just want to know, I said.

We stood in silence before the obstinate plant that would not yield any fruit. Then he knock-knocked on the top of my head with his knuckles. *We should go indoors or you'll catch the sun.*

Before I could roll my eyes, he let out a little snort. I rolled my eyes anyway and we both allowed ourselves a snigger. He always sniggers when people tell him to keep me indoors, lest I 'catch the sun'.

The only way I'll ever catch the sun is if the sun falls out of the sky and comes at me like a cricket ball coming over our boundary wall. I was born in the blazing afternoon heat, right here on the estate. I can take a lot of sun. My grandfather knows but he says it anyway, just to watch me roll my eyes or stamp my foot.

My smallest, most precious thing. I can't let the sun get you.

I waited until he had finished saying the whole thing, then I took a deep breath and said it out loud. Abu doesn't want to work the land. He says it's pointless because we cannot take the land with us when we leave.

Dada's fingers began to hover over the banana flower, as if he were soothing it. Telling it to go ahead and bloom; not to worry, we are not going anywhere. Then he knock-knocked the top of my head again and made that phup-phup sound between his lips.

Poor boy.

I glared. Poor boy! Abu is the one who does whatever he likes. You sent him so far, right across the country, for his master's degree. You spend so much money for him. Even in the holidays, he doesn't do anything. Not one single thing. He's always loitering on Mall Road, reading novels. He is not even studying his course material. He always reads out of syllabus. And he eats whenever, whatever. No timing. He hasn't set foot on the plantation for two months. He doesn't even come outside to look at the pepper vines that he helped train last summer. He hasn't even stepped out to see whether his banana trees have got more fruit than mine. I've been watering his trees all year. Why is he a poor boy?

I was about to say all of this out loud but then I remembered that Dada already knew. He had been urging my brother all of last week to go to the plantation.

Just go and look at the workers. Greet them, offer a salaam. Cast an eye on what is yours. I am holding it in trust for you. You and Fareeda.

Abu wouldn't budge. He sat at the table, running his hands through his curls like he's God knows what. His head cocked to one side, like he was considering the request. As if he was some petty official in the collectorate and as if our grandfather was a poor supplicant, standing before him with a bowed head. I could have kicked Abu that day.

Dada turned back towards the house. I hung back. I prefer to talk to him outdoors, in the sunshine. Once we are inside the house, it is impossible to talk freely. Especially if my brother is around. Sitting with some magazine. Lying down more likely. Mariam says he wakes up after ten most mornings and eats breakfast when it is time for lunch. He takes two hours just to read the newspaper. Sometimes he stares at his phone all afternoon. Then, just when it is time for Dada to return from his rounds of the estate, Abu washes up, gets dressed and goes out. Then he stays out the whole evening.

Dada noticed that I wasn't following and he turned around. I was still drawing circles in the mud with the tip of my shoe.

Loafer, I said. That's what he has become. Loafer! He doesn't want to work. It's just an excuse, isn't it? That it is coming and he can see it coming?

Our grandfather listened, his head bowed so I didn't have to look him in the eyes. I was grateful for that but I wished he would make some gesture that told me he knew what I was talking about. He was standing so still. I pressed on.

It's that phone of his. Phone groups. He says there's a group, all these people are on it. They are asking for special status as the true inhabitants of the land. They post a lot of pictures. They all dress up and bring out their guns and then they pose for photographs and send it out to everyone with a message. Like, be proud. Do or die. All the small and medium farmers are part of that group. Except for us. They don't invite our people to join.

Our people... Our people—

I hurried to cut him off. You know what I mean! Few of us own land. Not in this part of the district. Most of our people have shops, and the ones who do have plantations are far away. At least ten, fifteen kilometres off. I asked Abu how he found out about all this. Are

12

they saying things about us on this phone group? But he wouldn't tell me. I have sources, he says. What does he mean by that, 'sources'? That's just loafer talk. Isn't it?

I looked up at my grandfather, too quick for him to run a sleeve across his face and wipe it clean of all clues, and I caught a glint of something in his eyes. Then my heart was suddenly racing. Not even racing. More like it was ticking hard, like a bomb about to go off. Like last week, when Yashika and Deepika had pinned me to the wall. Their laughing mouths. Their teeth reminded me of the bone knives we saw on that field trip to the museum.

Dada stretched out his arm and tucked me into his side. We walked like that to the back of the house and entered through the kitchen door. We have walked like this since I was seven or eight.

Mariam says I have been glued to his waist for longer than that, ever since I was born. As soon as I could sit up, he had started to carry me on his hip. Before that, he strapped me to his back like the women who bring their babies to work on the plantation. He never asked Mariam or any of our relatives to take care of me, not even to bathe or change my nappies. He would say, *God has willed me to be a mother in my old age.*

Mariam had put our tea and murukku on the kitchen table and she had left for the day. We washed our hands and sat down. I bit into a murukku and through its

13

pleasant crunch, I mumbled, Dada, what happens if we eat pork?

He looked at me from under his white eyebrows. He was not smiling. He blew on the rim of his steel tumbler and took a cautious sip. Lukewarm, as he knew it would be, but he can never stop blowing at the rim first. My brother's caught the habit from him.

Nothing happens to the body. These people eat. Our neighbours. Workers. Forest men. They used to hunt wild boar. It's a huge beast. Very strong. Not easy to kill. Not like goat or sheep. They ate it. Many people eat. In foreign countries, I hear, the pigs are pink. You must have seen pictures in your storybooks. The pigs around town don't look so nice. Grey. Black, from rooting in the gutters. Don't feel like eating them, do you? But, well, I don't suppose they are, as such, well, their meat is not poisonous. It may give worms in the stomach.

He proceeded to take his usual big, loud slurp but his eyes never left me. *Why do you ask, my little baby?*

I broke a murukku in two, then broke the two parts into four. One-fourth of a part into two again. I put a thin sliver between my two front teeth. I didn't eat it, I said. I mean, I didn't swallow. I spat it out.

He laced his fingers around the tumbler, waited for me to look up. I kept my eyes fixed on the murukku, crumbling it into smaller bits.

Annie Zaidi

They mixed it into the rice. They said, *It's our special type of biryani.* It didn't smell or anything. I didn't know, Dada. I don't know what it tastes like. Yashika was there and it was from her cousin's tiffin. They said, *Try it, try it.* So I ate one spoon of rice. Then they said, *Try the meat too, you must try it with the meat.* So I took another spoonful. And then those other girls came and stood around. Deepika and her group. She's the one I don't like. And Yashika's cousin, he was staring at me. It felt funny. The meat was not like our usual meat. It was like a glob of fat. Like some resin had been melted down. There was no taste in my mouth. I tried to spit it out into my palm. But then Yashika and Deepika—

I reached out for my tumbler of tea but Dada caught my hand in his. He began to dust off the murukku crumbs from my palm.

Yashika too, eh?

I nodded. They had grabbed my hands and they were laughing. Then I guessed. Looking at their faces, I guessed. They were telling me, now eat it properly. They were holding my hands down. Like this. One on each side. I kept trying to chew, then I just spat it out. It fell on the front of my tunic. They said, *yuck yucky yuck!* Then Yashika's cousin said, *See? I told you! She won't.*

I was not crying but Dada lifted my palm to his lips and kissed it like he used to when I was howling. That

15

was when I was little. He didn't let go of my hand as he picked up another murukku. He took a bite and fed me the rest with his own hand. I reached for my tumbler and drained my tea in one gulp.

Dada, you know what? Your Abubaker has gone to the big city and he has turned into a big donkey. But I am here. I'll manage the estate. I don't have any obsession for university. Studying and studying and studying. For what?

Well, your brother wants to be a college professor. You have to study many years to become that.

I harrumphed. Who knows if he actually wants to be a professor? Political Science, he says, but I only see him reading novels and poems.

Dada smiled. This was his favourite topic. *A book is a book. It does not hurt to read stories and poems. They give you knowledge of people's hearts, which is the most precious knowledge of all.*

But, I protested, he doesn't even learn that much. He keeps giving and taking books from Devaki. She went off and got married, and still he's going to her house to borrow storybooks. Stupid boy!

Before our grandfather could reply, I pushed back my chair. Yes, yes, I know! I never say these things outside. I'm just telling you. Mariam also knows. She says that Devaki is a gone case. She also sent a book of poems through Mariam and you know what she said? *Fareeda might enjoy it.* You should have heard Mariam laugh. Straightaway she went and put the book near Abu's pillow.

Dada leaned back in his chair and sighed, then he sighed again. *Poor boy!*

He said nothing else for the rest of the day. I was feeling much lighter, having told him. But later that night, when I was doing my homework, he came into my room. He sat down and watched me work. My brother, as usual, was out gallivanting somewhere. Dada picked up my school diary. Not to check it. Just turned the pages. Even when my class teacher sends a disciplinary note home, he doesn't read it. It is up to me to inform him whether I've been naughty at school.

I was bent over my notebook. I had to write three hundred words on the political imperatives leading up to the Partition. Capital P, as Garuda sir says. I was only forty-three words down.

What is the homework?

It's rubbish homework, I muttered. Dada didn't say anything and I thought, sheesh! Now I am starting to sound like Abu. I straightened up.

It's from modern Indian history, I said. I have to write about the first half of the twentieth century, the years before we got freedom.

Dada's eyes lit up. He had been only five years old when we got freedom but he claims to remember the day. I was worried that now he would start telling me the whole story again. So I bent my head, pen pressing down on the paper, and waited. But for a long minute, he didn't say a word. Then he came close to me and kissed my forehead.

Listen. If it ever happens again—God willing it will not happen again—but if it does, don't fight. Just eat it.

18

10-B Mass Flunks a Snap Test

Good afternoon. No reading today. Close your books. Close them, put them away in the desk.

Yashika! Do you need a handwritten invitation to put away your book, madam? Should the invitation card be embossed with the school seal?

So! First question. The First Battle of Panipat was fought between who and who? Raise your hands. Do I see a hand?

Wrong! Not between Rana Pratap and Akbar. Where is Panipat? Anyone?

Class 10-B! Where is Panipat?

Yes, we now call it Haryana. Who was in charge of Haryana then?

Shame, shame, shame. Who ruled Delhi in the

fourteenth century?

I am dying out here. Help me. Please. Someone.

How many days have we been doing medieval history? We just finished reading about the Second Battle of Panipat and you have already forgotten the first battle. Public memory is indeed short.

No! It was not fought between the Mughals and Marathas. You're jumping the gun. The First Battle of Panipat was fought between Ibrahim Lodi and Babur, who was not, properly speaking, a 'Mughal'. His people were originally from Central Asia, from the Chagatai tribe. He had some Turkish blood, but Central Asian means what? Mongol. But when he came to India, people began to say, Mughal.

It's like when you go to the USA, over there people will ask: *You speak Indoo?* What they actually mean to ask is, do you speak Hindi? Because they think *Indoo* is all we've got in India. Now maybe you can speak Hindi but it is not your mother tongue, so you will say: No! But after some time, one more person will ask: *You speak Indoo?* Again you say, NO! Then one more person will ask, and you start to think, what the hell! Just say yes.

So Babur came here and settled down. He probably thought, what the hell. Call me Mughal, it's fine. Call me anything, it's fine. The weather is great. The wine is top class. What's in a name?

Annie Zaidi

So! Who won the Second Battle of Panipat?

Not Babur, Fareeda. The SECOND battle. Come on, my young compatriots. I'll give you a hint: a Mughal was involved.

Oh my thirty-three million gods! Just this week, we have read about the Second Battle of Panipat. Say something!

Not Humayun. It was Akbar. Akbar fought—? Ah! I spy a raised hand.

Correct. Hemchandra Vikramaditya, lovingly called Hemu. Who gave him this pet name, nobody knows. What was Hemu fighting for?

For himself, of course. But for someone else, technically speaking. See, Akbar had to re-establish control over Delhi. Not establish, mind you, but re-establish. Or rather, re-re-establish. His father, Humayun, had been defeated once by—?

Thank you, Deepika. At least you remembered one third of his name. Suri. But it was not the famous Suri that you are thinking about. Sher Shah Suri had defeated Humayun and taken control of Delhi. Then a lot of things happened. Conspiracy. Murder. Child murder. Patricide, fratricide, regicide. Please meet me in the library on Saturday in case you are interested in all the gory details. We have a long and glorious history of every colour and shape of homicide.

Prelude to a Riot

Anyway. Humayun took Delhi back from the Suri kings. But then Humayun died. Akbar was a boy-king. Thirteen years old. Younger than you all. He must have looked something like the students from the eighth standard. Can you imagine that? Anyway, so Delhi was lost, and this time it was taken by Adil Shah Suri. But he was also busy trying to win another battle in Bengal, against—?

We read this last week. It was Mohammad Shah, in Bengal. Our Hemu was Adil Shah's right-hand man. Chief of the armed forces. So Hemu managed to take back the throne of Delhi, technically on behalf of Adil Shah Suri. But loyalty is in inverse proportion to ambition. Since Hemu was winning battles, Hemu said, oho! Why should I not be king? Well, he was only able to sit on the throne for less than a month. In the Second Battle of Panipat, Hemu was defeated, beheaded, et cetera.

Who was leading the battle on Akbar's side? Remember, Akbar was quite a young boy. He was not in a position to fight for himself. Should I expect an answer?

I see. Open your books and check.

It was Ali Quli Khan Shaibani. Not to be confused with Ali Quli Istajlu, also known as Sher Afghan Khan, first husband of the future empress, Noor Jehan. There is a difference of one generation between the two Ali Quli gents. Now, turn to page 132 please.

Annie Zaidi

An Anonymous Poem is Published in the Newspaper

*I*t was not a matter of blind

*C*hance that you were sent where I was

*H*ere, twenty days apart, we were planted

*O*thers tell me, I was the answer to my mother's prayers

*O*thers tell you, you slid out of your mother's womb

*S*miling, but you do not believe them

*E*ver heard the story of why children are born without

*L*anguage? It is so that they may not reveal the truth

*O*f God and the angels to mere mortals

*V*ery little of God remains by the time language snags
  our lips

*E*ver wondered what secrets you knew that you came heels

*O*ver head and smiling all the way out into a
*V*elvety purple June night
*E*yes filled with diamonds that have learnt to
*R*icochet like bullets, off silent walls?
*A*nd surely you knew, I was here too
*N*ot four miles away?
*D*id you not chortle and clap your hands
A hundred times a day
*B*ecause you remembered the promises we made before
  God?
*O*thers tell me, I was born tongue-tied and was
*V*exed by the need to make words in order to be heard
*E*xcept with you, who already knew.

24   @ABC

Annie Zaidi

Devaki's Soliloquy

Meera writes in her new novel that stories of love and tears make her puke. She has written a lot about cadavers this time. It is about a fascination rather than a love story.

When Abu came to return the book, he kept staring out of the window. There is nothing to look at, just a stretch of patchy grass and the boundary wall. Not even a sorry cactus plant. I cannot make anything bloom in this garden, I told him.

He stayed quiet. I knew what he wanted to say. When we were free to speak our minds, he would not have hesitated.

Come home. Learn from my grandfather how to grow things. Dada can make rocks bleed green.

Then I would have said, oh no! Dada does not make rocks bleed. He bleeds himself until the earth gives him a reward. Men like your grandfather have sacrificed themselves to the land. Blood and sweat. They don't just supervise the sweat flowing down other people's backs.

I know why Abu was staring out of the window. It was so he didn't have to look at my face. I too stared outside, so I could stop looking at him. The air was thick with the juice of the words we had locked behind our teeth.

I envy you, I said at last. You can read Meera in the original. He shrugged.

Meera doesn't care. You can read her in any language, she's just as good. She's the great Meera. And who are we?

He glanced at me when he said those words. *Who are we?* Then, too quick, he turned his gaze back to the window.

It was unbearable. I returned to the safe island of literature and accents. The way your language sounds, I said, I am comforted by its rattle. It is as if all the sharp corners of life have been rounded out by your forefathers and placed on your tongue. When you speak in your language, especially when I hear you talking about your little sister, your words appear soft, like the touch of baby skin.

He smiled at that but he didn't take his eyes off the

window. Then, at last, he said it.

You put in glass shards.

The setting sun glinted off the yellow and brown bits of glass cemented onto the top of the garden wall. Yes, I admitted. Saju insisted. Well, it wasn't really Saju. It was my father. He comes here and keeps talking about break-ins. He says you can't trust people nowadays. Things are getting worse. The hired hands are not locals. I mean, the local tribes are different. They would not, I mean, that's what Appa says.

Abu nodded but his hands were restless. It was as if he would prefer that I didn't speak. He didn't want to hear about Appa. He's heard all this before. Still. I felt compelled to explain the glass shards.

They come from beer bottles. Two hundred and nine bottles. Collected over this summer. We used to, well, I used to give them away to the recycling man. He comes by every Tuesday. But he—Vinny, that is—I don't know what came over him. One day he just picked up the empty bottles and started smashing them against the wall. Just like that. Without any provocation at all! Just smashsmashsmash.

I was shaking again. I had been shaking that day when they were smashing the bottles. Vinny started it, then Appa joined in. Saju too. They were bent over and laughing by the end of it.

I felt like I had to sit down. I said, let's sit. Please Abu, sit for a while.

He wouldn't sit. He wouldn't stay for tea. He said he would return when Saju was at home. This time, he didn't ask where Saju was. I know that he knows. Saju is at the bakery until seven every evening. Abu knows that I know that he already knows this.

I walked him out. His eyes remained fixed on the ground as he unlatched the gate and latched it again. Then he started to walk away. One step, two steps. I felt as if a cold, leaden river of blood was turning to ice around my heart. I called out his name. Abu returned to the gate.

Vinny's got a new gun, I said. A small one. The range is better, he says. He's bought it in his wife's name. He says he has to worry about her security. Because he is out so often. He goes on and on about security. Bavna's security, my security.

Abu stood leaning on the gate. Not one word. I wanted to grab his collar and shake him. I wanted to say, Abu, why don't you get a gun licence too? Get a small gun. Get it for Fareeda. Doesn't she need security? But I didn't say it.

His hand stayed on the latch. For a moment I thought he might change his mind, and step indoors again. But of course, he did not. Before he left, he looked up, straight into my eyes. *Remember to tell Saju that I came by.*

He won't come for a week now. Won't sit and eat my food. Not any more.

No, not mine. It's Saju's food that he won't eat. Saju's house, Saju's food.

Appa's house. Appa's food. When I lived there, I used to think, I don't want to eat in this house. I have not eaten in Appa's house since I managed to get away from it. But there's no getting away, is there?

Appa has two rifles. Vinny already had a rifle, the one he inherited from our grandfather. Now he's gone and bought the handgun. Bavna can't even thread a needle on her own. No chance she'll ever learn to shoot. What's that word? Stockpile?

I asked Appa once, how many hands does he have? Is he some four-armed deity that he can use two arms to load and two to fire two rifles simultaneously? He had scowled.

We're a martial people. We have always kept guns. It is in our culture. Even the white rulers accepted it. They never stopped us from carrying guns.

Appa had once flung a pot of hot rice across the dining table. That was after I had said that if our guns were recognized by white rulers, then we must have done something to please them. Didn't that make us traitors? Appa had shouted. *Not us! They were the traitors.*

29

And what treachery were they guilty of? I had shouted back. They refused to genuflect to the white man, that's their crime?

That's when the pot of rice had come spinning towards my end of the table. Three hot grains landed on my lap. A hot gob of rice landed on Amma's forearm and she hissed from between her teeth.

Us and them. Them and us.

Three hundred years ago, our clan sided with the whites. My ancestors helped them bring down a brown king. How many times I've heard the story. How *we* helped get rid of *him*. The British gave us guns. Us, not them. Ever since, we have had the upper hand. Guns against swords. Except, we have swords, too. Two swords in my own household. They are polished every year.

Appa loves to tell the story of the British felling Tipu Sultan. He used to tell it six, seven times a month when I was still living with them. Now he tells it six days a week, in my home.

Why did these people convert? Even if they did, at least they should remember that they did not change their faith willingly. No, no, never willingly! It was through the sword.

When I was in college, I used to argue with him. I'd say, Appa, conversion means someone is unhappy. If people gain freedom, happiness, anything, even money, why should they not convert? It is the right thing to do.

How does it matter—name, shape of headgear, dress?

Appa would say that college was putting dung inside my head. I would say, no, college was taking the dung out of my head. On and on. Me versus him.

Three hundred years' worth of stories, clogging up the arteries of our men. Sitting tight around their hearts, slimy and thick with half-truths. It makes the dinner table noxious. My father, my brother. Now Saju too. Saju, who used to say things like, victory is only half the story.

If one feels like a winner, he will make sure the other fellow feels like a loser. People change, but only to suit their convenience. Nobody submits to any new thing easily— king, custom, science. Not unless they are faced with fear, or favour. A king conquers a place and all the people become his people. They can take his faith and his favour, or they can rebel. Rally behind a new candidate. And if they choose to rebel, that too is for selfish reasons. What is there to feel proud about killing for the sake of faith? It is not a great act of peace or charity.

We used to talk in this way. Saju, me, Abu.

A king with the heart of a lion, and we felled him. We! Whatever we gained from the whites, there was blood on our hands. With a great roar, he fell. Died fighting. A king who goes down fighting is a true king.

Saju used to say these things, and he would slap his chest as he said, *Lion-man!* As if he were a lion-man himself.

Prelude to a Riot

Kings, flags, poems. It was Saju who pointed out that the clothes my people wear to weddings, the outfit Appa puts on for his weekend meetings, are not so far from the clothes the Mughals used to wear. Long sleeves, double-breasted tunic, tight pyjamas, a sash. These are historic clues, Saju used to say. There was very little difference between us in our ways of life.

The big difference was, our people turned upon a brown man, and we allowed the whites to take control. That was a kind of treason. That was Saju's word. Treason.

If those guys were fighting, fighting with the strength of their arms, winning wars for one thousand years, north-south, east-west, then they deserved to be kings. No? Then who is the more deserving martial race? Obviously! If being a martial race entitles you to keep guns, then those guys, these descendants of Mughals and Pathans, should have the right to drive around in military tanks! Logic and common sense, isn't it?

I used to take his arguments home. I would unwrap them at the dining table. If our cultures are so different, I'd say to Appa, then why is your traditional dress like *their* traditional dress? If we are a local tribe, as you say, then why are you not wearing a tiny loincloth like the tribals who live in the forests? If our culture matters so much, why don't we bury the dead like our forefathers used to? Grandmother asked to be buried, didn't she?

Annie Zaidi

You say we must preserve our culture, our traditions. So then you should go and tell everyone that our clan does not support the burning of our dead. Burning the dead is alien to us. It represents the hegemony of other invading clans. Dare you say it?

Appa would get that look on his face, like he was thinking that someone should slap me hard but he didn't want to do it himself. Vinny and Bavna would go quiet and pull sombre faces, like I had said a dirty word without knowing its meaning. My mother's tongue, shielding me.

Shut up and eat. Why can't you all eat in silence?

I shut up. Every time. My heart would be beating loud. I was seventeen and grateful that somebody had told me to shut up just in time. One more word and I would have got a thrashing.

I have never been properly thrashed. Perhaps this is the problem. I need to grow a thicker skin. Saju says it too. *Too much pampering.*

Too many dresses. Too many times Amma had to say, shut up and eat. I always heeded her warning. I should have let him thrash me. I would have stopped caring. Two slaps. Five kicks. Over the years, I would have become immune. Thick skin.

Two years ago, Saju and I knew how to talk. I could tell him, forget all this. Those were different times. Brown fought brown. White fought white. Everyone fights for land, tax, religion. It's just power play. One man gets knocked off the throne by the next fellow. Big deal!

Saju was not like Appa. That was the main thing. Saju's father came here wearing all his differences on his body. Different smelling hair oil. Different style of draping cloth over his legs. Different code of love. His mother had fallen for his father. They married in secret. We had gone to his father's farm for a picnic once. Abu, me, Saju. It was more beautiful than it is here. Flat fields. Placid, green waters. Abu told me that his great-great-grandfather had also come from a village like that.

Saju, me, Abu. Me walking between the two of them. A hundred bursts of laughter every hour. Walking back from college, standing outside Town Hall for five minutes, then five minutes longer. Never wanting to go home. That's what I loved most. Saju, me, Abu.

It is Appa's doing. When I told them at home that I'll marry this boy, I didn't really know what I wanted. But Appa said he would never allow it. Vinny too. *The clan will disown you. You will not get one square inch of land, not one gram of gold, nothing!*

It was because of those aunts and uncles who showed up, telling Appa to lock me up in my room. The way those goons showed up at the wedding mandap, saying you can't do this or that ritual. *These are sacred rituals, not meant for outsiders.*

Annie Zaidi

They had pushed Saju at the wedding mandap and it was only then that I felt the grip of a strong talon around my heart. Only then did I feel that I must marry this man, and no one else. Until that day, all I knew was that I wanted to capture that feeling of the three of us—Abu, me, Saju—sitting near the lake, looking at the green water. I knew I couldn't possibly cling to it much longer. After I graduated, I wouldn't be able to stay out all day.

Bavna had warned. *You'll see. It passes. It ends. Like that.*

She had snapped her fingers so close to my nose that I had flinched. I thought that she meant my marriage to Saju would not last. So I had hissed back. No! You will see! We will last longer than you and Vinny, I had declared. But now I wonder if she meant something else?

It ends. Like that.

I could breathe as long as they kept their distance. Then Vinny walked in one evening, one beer tower tucked under each armpit. Never asked for my permission. Just walked into the house, calling out for Saju. Appa came later. More bottles. Then it began. Them and us. Us and them. All our troubles, all their ease.

For two years, I breathed easy. After the wedding, Appa wouldn't set foot in this house. He used to slow down at the gate but he never got out of the jeep. Saju would step outside, fold his hands politely. Appa would mumble a word or two about the estate, the prices of pepper, bananas, and the workers who were crossing all limits. Then he would spit in the dust.

Mobile phones! Imagine? These buggers! What do they need phones for, to ring the monkeys in the forest? Huh! Didn't have a rag to cover their assholes, did they? Now just look at them. Jeans! And phone in the back pocket. And the radio singing to their bums while they work. Hah! Now these new workers, all illegal of course. Don't you think? They say they're from the east. But everyone knows they come from across the border. But for all the mustard oil they slop up, they're cheap hands. Bloody illegals. See what we have been reduced to?

36   I could hear him, standing at the kitchen window. Still. It didn't matter so much as long as he stayed outside. Everybody says such things and my Appa has never been a paragon of peace or empathy. But once Vinny stepped into the house with his beer towers, it was over. Now he comes every other day. Winking at Saju, nodding at me as if he was doing me a big favour. As if this was not my house too. As if I were just a servant working in the kitchen. Then Appa started gracing us with his forgiving presence. Saju stopped folding his hands.

I stew. Dinner is pushed back. Later and later. Beer. Banana chips. Tongues working hard.

I hide in the kitchen. I water the plants in the garden.

I iron clothes with headphones in my ears. But no matter how far I retreat, Appa's voice finds me. Hissing, spitting. Us. Them. Them. Us. Nothing blossoms in my garden.

One of them has bought a new jeep.

One of them has a three-storeyed house.

One of them has a new shop opposite the fort.

One of them is getting his daughter married and giving her kilos of gold.

One of them is going to the Gulf. All of them go to the Gulf. Slick, black, greasy Arab money and they're fattening up on it. They don't even need plantations. We put in plants, so much money on soil and fertilizer and pesticide and hiring these hands. What do we make?

What do you make, Saju? I've got land, but do I have a three-storeyed house? See? I don't have a son in the Gulf. This wife of yours, my daughter, is she covered in gold?

Have you seen the road above the wine shop, the one Bavna's father owns? Every other shop there is a jewellery shop. Where does the money come from? I'll tell you. It's from the underworld. These people, they're all connected.

My head pounds. After Appa and Vinny leave, I put dinner on the table. I call Saju to come eat. He comes. The beer towers, the three-storeyed houses, the gold I did not bring with me: I can see it swilling in his bloodshot eyes.

I can't help it. I start babbling. I put forward a counter

list. Saju's niece is moving to London for higher studies, no scholarship. She's not going to do something useful like law or engineering. She's going to study art history. Where does she get the money for nonsense foreign studies? His mother's side of the family is rich. Aren't they rich?

I press on. Saju's parents bought a bakery to set us up after the wedding. No bank loans. Just gave him the money. Go, run a bakery or whatever you want. He wanted a modern cafe, not these old-fashioned sit-eat-get-lost kind of bakeries like Royal. Now Saju has the best location, halfway up the hill where all the young people hang out; right on the main road, walking distance from our college, but far from the town market, so there is no danger of running into parents. So where did his parents find so much money to pay for the property and the fancy decor?

I can see he does not want to hear it. All these young people who are spending money every day at your cafe, what about them? Is that Gulf money? And are we not cutting into Royal's business? When we were in college, we used to go to Royal all the time. We spent hours there, nursing a cup of coffee. Now college students who have extra money have stopped hanging out at Royal. They come to you instead. So should the old bakeries start crying? Should they ask: where did Saju get the money to make such a fancy cafe?

Annie Zaidi

And gold? You should ask Appa. For Vinny's wedding, my mother bought all the gold jewellery right here, in the same local shops. I bring up Bavna's new gold bracelets. She's just bought a new pair. If Appa and Vinny are not making money, then how is Bavna getting new gold sets? Is she robbing the gold shops or is the underworld sending her gifts?

I can sense my upper lip curling when I say that word. Underworld. Saju swats the air, as if he were swatting away a fly or mosquito. I know what the gesture means. An urge to use his hands, to swat my voice away.

I twist my mouth, plough on. Appa has grand plans for expanding his homestay into a resort. Not one, not two, five new cottages have been built on his estate. Can't I see where the money is flowing like water? As for his workers! If one shirt is filthy, the other one is wet. Sucking their blood, then abusing them—this is our culture?

I can feel my nostrils starting to flare. Does Appa ask which side of the border they come from when he's bargaining like the devil himself to pay just half the government rate? One piece of checked cloth around their hips and they look like terrorists, eh? But look at who is buying all the guns! Which underworld is funding our guns?

Saju tells me to shut up. The day before, he said

it. *You talk too bloody much. Why don't you just shut up and eat?*

I shut up. I stuffed my mouth until my eyes began to sting.

Bavna's fingers were snapping, one inch from my nose. *It won't last.*

Amma's voice, warning. *Shut up and eat. Or don't eat. Let us eat in peace.*

I used to fantasize about the day I would not shut up. Instead, I would turn around and say to my mother, Amma, if you have any guts, why don't you tell Appa to shut up and eat? He is the one who talks too much.

Foolish girl. Amma's gone. Never said a word to Appa as long as she lived.

That night, after Saju told me to shut up, I finished all the rice on my plate. All the meat, salad, everything. I got up from the table and washed my hands and plate at the kitchen sink. I went into the living room, turned on the TV and watched the news until midnight. Saju came to ask if I wasn't going to sleep. I muted the sound on the TV without turning around to look at him. I just sat on the sofa and stared at the soundless TV screen until Saju had fallen asleep. Or rather, until he started pretending.

I know he pretends. He is waiting to see how long I can keep this up. If I'll come and lie beside him, allow him to act like it's nothing. Two days. Three days.

I used to read books after dinner, in bed. I didn't wait for him to leave for work in the morning before picking up a book. These days, I worry. He might say, *You read too bloody much*. And then I will not be able to touch books in this house. I will feel like I am soiling the book.

The news makes no sense if you turn the sound off. The ticker at the bottom of the screen only tells stock market rates.

Abu says the stock market is also important. Stock market falls, government could fall. But it's not falling now. The arrow is green and pointing upwards. The anchor's nails are polished. Transparent polish. Or pearl colour.

Bavna's fingers snapsnap before my nose, as if she's trying to yank me out of a dream. But there's nothing to yank me out of. I feel yanked out, but I enter no other version of reality. There is no air here. Not even a vacuum. Just snapsnap and flinch.

An Advertisement Appears in the Newspaper

Immediate Sale: Plantation, 1.5 acres. Over 100 fruit trees. Crop will be left standing.

Call: xxxxx xxxxx. Only serious enquiry.

Saju's Soliloquy

So what wrong thing did I say? Isn't it a fact?

It is the third mosque in town. If it is not the first and it is not the second, then it has to be the third. Right or wrong?

Nothing wrong with stating a simple fact. But the way she's reacting, it's as if I've gone and beaten somebody up. Just like her clan had come to beat me up at the wedding. Now she has the guts to tell me how to talk.

You should think of who is listening, how he might be feeling.

Hog's cunt, his feelings! As if I should be thinking and weighing each word. In my own cafe too! Sheh! Anyway, why should his feelings be hurt when I am stating a fact? It's not like I invited him to come there and then deliberately started counting mosques.

He was sitting at his usual table, the one near the counter. We can talk that way while I continue to work. Then Vinny and Appa also came. And why shouldn't they? They are my family now. They know Abu is my friend. Their daughter's college friend. So, of course, they were not going to sit at another table. Why should they not sit down at the same table and have a chat with my friends?

That was the day they were going to get Vinny a new revolver. Appa already has two guns. But Vinny wanted a licensed handgun. He says, small guns are best. You can take them with you at night. Easy, keep it discreet. Glove compartment, or under the driver's seat, or inside a handbag. The wife can use it too. If she ever learns, that is.

Not much chance of that happening. Bavna hasn't even learnt to drive a car yet. Still, a gun is useful for emergencies, even if it is just to frighten some of these people. Workers get ideas. There might be burglars. Whoever. A small handgun could be useful. That's how the topic came up. Appa asked if I had visited the gun shop recently. I said, no, never.

Ah! Have you seen the new mosque they're building, right behind the gun shop? It's coming up on that empty plot where the boys used to play cricket. It used to belong to

Annie Zaidi

Abu's father's maternal aunt. He would know more details, of course.

Appa was looking at Abu, waiting. He expected some kind of response. Something! But Abu just sat there, staring at the coconut clementines in the display counter.

It makes my head hot. The way he comes in and sits down, hardly talking. Looks around at the tables, at the baked stuff, here and there. It's almost like he's come to check me out, what is Saju up to? Sheh! If he has nothing to say, why hang around? Is there a lack of bakeries in this town?

So I just said it, casual like. That makes it the third mosque in town, no? That's it. Just that. And it is true. There is the old white mosque, near the bridge. Then there's the small one behind Royal Bakery. Now this one will be the third. And I am not even counting the big green one that's near the highway.

As if anyone is keeping count. There must be a dozen mosques in the district by now. Anyway, I didn't start talking about the whole district. I just stated a simple fact, that this will be the third mosque in town. But Devaki says, you may have hurt his feelings.

He's a sly one though, isn't he? Sitting quiet as a mouse in front of me, but then going and talking to Devaki. See what all is being said by your people. In the cafe, there wasn't one squeak out of him. He sat with me and my in-laws but he would not even look at us. He kept moving his thumbs about in circles, and staring at his own feet in those dirty sandals. Sheh!

I don't know why Abu can't get a pair of good shoes. If his grandfather has the money to keep him in university, five years after finishing college, he can afford to buy a decent pair of shoes. Why would anyone dress like a beggar?

Maybe he thinks that if people see him in those rotten sandals, they will not know how much the old man has got stashed away. I once asked. Just casual like, what rate are you all getting for pepper this year? He shrugged me off.

I don't take an interest in the plantation any more.

As if there's anybody who doesn't take an interest in money. Sheh! Sly fellows. Vinny was right about one thing. No matter how well you think you know them, they'll never be open and free with you. The other day, Abu comes here and starts lecturing me.

Didn't you ever want to study further? Didn't you want to do your master's? You wanted to do law, remember?

He thinks I don't understand why he's talking of further studies. He bought an entrance form for Devaki. Bachelor's in Education. So she can get a teaching job somewhere. She's also not being straight with me. Didn't show me the form until yesterday, when she needed to pay the fees.

I've been thinking about it for a year. I should do something. House and all is fine. I can study and do housework. Or I'll hire a woman to help. There won't be any dust. I'll manage all the cooking. I always wanted to be a teacher. You have a problem?

Fifteen different things she said, but she didn't say where and when she got that form. The form came from the university. University means four hours drive, going there and coming back. So when did she get it? Did it arrive by post?

Then it came out. Abu bought the form. He was concerned. My housewife is wasting her talent. And she insisting. *I was the one who asked him to bring the form.*

As if anyone wants to stop her. Study, I told her. Study through distance education. But you can't travel four hours every day. God knows how many hours you will have to sit in classes. Those who do such professional courses, they usually live on campus.

Her face. She was silent, eyes down, but I could see. She's already thought about this. I saw it on her face. She thinks she might go and live on the university campus. I told her right then. She can work with me if the housework is too boring for her. Girls work in cafes in all the big towns these days. Or she can study long distance. But not this crazy type of commute.

Prelude to a Riot

Madam wants to go to university. Why now? Eight years I've known her, and she never said that she wants to be a teacher. As if I don't know who put this in her head.

Fine, Devaki and I got friendly because of him. Okay. I'll give him that much. He used to come to my house, drink tea. He talked to my parents. Okay, fine. Even now he comes and goes. But he goes and brings university forms for her, then he sits in my cafe with his beaten-dog look. Spoils the atmosphere. Here I am, trying to make a certain type of cafe. Clean. Bright. Yellow and blue walls. No hurry like, drink coffee and get lost. I don't go and slap a bill on the table when young people are chit-chatting. The customers wear nice clothes. But here is this man with dirty sandals. Forget the atmosphere of the place, he just spoils my mood.

That day, as soon as Vinny and Appa left, he also took off. He told me he wanted to go and buy some books. But half an hour later, when I went down to the supplier for my cakes, there he was. Standing outside the small mosque, drinking tea. He was chatting with his own people. I bet he went to sit in Royal afterwards.

To hell with him. Not like I don't keep the same cake and pastry. He can go eat wherever. And Devaki can sniff and skulk in the kitchen if she wants to, sleep in the TV room if she wants to. I prefer that to her whining.

Annie Zaidi

Why doesn't Abu come over for dinner? Why don't you invite Abu over at home? Why don't we go and meet Dada some day?

Dada! As if Abu's grandfather was her grandfather too. And for her own father and brother, she has no respect.

Why do they land up here every evening? Why is Vinny obsessed with guns?

As if he's going to point the gun at her head! Vinny is right about this. He says some women just don't have a logical mind. Better to keep them busy with kids and all. Only kids can sort their brains out. Permanently sorts them out. Well, at least for twenty years.

Devaki has no common sense. That day, one fellow came into our house. Bavna had sent one of the estate hands with a tiffin box. He didn't even have a shirt on. Half naked. Just a lungi around his waist and even that had a big hole at the back. I could see his underwear. He was barefoot, so I didn't hear his footsteps on the driveway. This stranger walks in out of the dark. No ringing the bell, no knocking. The door was ajar and he just walked in.

I was thinking, now here's a problem and I don't have a gun in the house. Not even a big knife at hand. And my Mrs? She folds her hands, goes up to him. Asks if he has eaten dinner. She asks for his name. He could not pronounce his own name properly. Mommad something.

Then something else. Half of this language, half of that language, half in sign language. Then she goes into the kitchen and brings out a jackfruit.

Thank you, Mommad. Please accept this. From me, for your children. We have a jackfruit tree. There are too many jackfruits and just the two of us here.

I asked her later. What, we are now on a first name basis with the field workers? She gave me that look, the look she gives Vinny sometimes.

We have always been on a first name basis with field workers. The workers, however, are not on a first name basis with us.

Then it starts. Her complaints about how Bavna sends the field workers over as if they were her personal servants, and not paying the workers one rupee extra for these extra errands. Her own sister-in-law is being generous to us. But never happy, this woman. Here she is getting a hot tiffin, full of juicy pork curry, but she is only bothered about some illegal from who knows where.

Better this way, I told her. They shouldn't start to feel too comfortable. Or entitled to extra tips and gifts. These workers who have been coming in the last season, you see the way they are squatting on public land, right outside plantations? Will they let go of the land so easily?

Devaki disappeared into the kitchen and kept up her nonsense from there.

Annie Zaidi

So, will the estate owners let them live on private land? If not on public land, where should they sleep and shit? In the treetops? Even that is not possible. Because you all own the trees too.

You all? Like, who all? I don't own any trees, I said. And there is no need to fight with me because of illegal workers. I am also sympathetic.

Don't call them illegal. You don't know that they're illegal.

Of course they are illegal, I said. Not one piece of paper to show, no proof of residence, no school certificate.

They drop out of school, so where will the certificates come from?

And what about that rascal who was caught with a minor girl, huh? No way to track these fellows down in case something happens. No identity cards. You are a woman, you should be concerned about the safety of girls at least, I told her. It could have been one of your nieces.

She started laughing then. Just stood there and laughed at my face.

Girls' safety, is it? No other argument left?

She can say anything but one hundred per cent, they are illegal. Only illegals are so desperate. They come so far, they don't speak the language, don't have a roof, not even a ditch to piss and shit in, but they stay and work at half the government rate. It's good business for men like Appa, that much is true. Appa curses them

51

morning and night, but he hires them. Problem is, they don't vanish conveniently after the harvest season is over. They hang around. Chase them off the land, they'll go to the mines. Season changes, and they're back for the planting. One of them finds a toehold and he pulls over another hundred.

Use your brains, I told Devaki. What do they need a new mosque for? New buildings means there has to be a new demographic. These people are prospering on our soil. Okay, fine. No problem. But your Appa has a point. Can we predict whether or not there is a terrorist or some radical type lurking behind a torn and faded lungi?

Whatever. She doesn't care. The only thing that matters to her is, Abu is sulking and this is my fault.

Why do you want to count mosques? Why don't you ever tell Vinny, let's talk about something else?

I told her nicely enough. See, I have a mouth. I will do what I like with it. And you also have a mouth. So you should learn to keep some control over it.

Just stating a simple fact. Sheh! Such drama. One of these days, she'll really get it from me.

Annie Zaidi

A Curious Advertisement

Wanted: Massage lady. 4 days work per week guaranteed. Pay per session + free meals.

Must be available Saturday, Sunday. Family environment. Ladies to ladies only. Decent ladies apply, professionals please excuse.

Bavna's Soliloquy

Time to go here, there, everywhere, but he doesn't have time to get the damn pipes fixed. I've told Vinny fifteen times that the kitchen sink is clogged up. But of course the kitchen is my responsibility, the sink is my domain!

Non-stop chatter. He collects gossip like an old woman. I can't sit and listen to him all day, so off he goes in the jeep. I tell him not to trouble me, off he goes to Devaki's. That's the latest.

Men are funny creatures, I swear. Such a hoo-ha at Devaki's wedding. People coming and going, everyone had a suggestion on how to break her down.

Lock her up and don't feed her for three days.

No, beat up that fellow, Saju. Teach him to marry out of caste.

We told you not to send her to a co-ed school. You should have sent her to a reputable girls' convent. Don't our girls also go out to study?

Should have whipped her into shape by now.

Now? Father and son, every other evening they are lolling about in Devaki's drawing room. They come back saying, he's not a bad fellow, eh? And not one word about the girl. Our own girl, mind you. When I ask, how is she, what did she do today? No answer.

She came to see me yesterday when these two were out in town for the rally. Stay for lunch, I said. I must have said it fifteen times. Stay! You're coming home after three years, I said. But no means no. Obstinate as a mule.

She didn't speak much. Just stood here in the kitchen, twisting the edge of her saree between her fingers. I had to supervise the cleaning of the cottages. So I said, come, you follow me and make yourself useful. Poor thing. She wandered about the rooms, touching things. Curtain. Table cover. Book. An old map of the district that used to hang in her old room. She took it off the wall and then kept folding and refolding it.

I asked her. Baby, is there a problem? I used to call her Baby. She was such a child when I first stepped into this household. Such a sweet, pointy face. Like a

55

kitten, with her wary grey eyes. Later, in her teens, she shot up. Grew a full hand taller than me. All these years later, the look on her face is exactly the same. Like she is judging you. She wants to come closer but she is not sure about your intent.

My first thought was, she must be pregnant. Or maybe she had a miscarriage. Three years, no news. I asked, but she shook her head. Still, I thought, it must be something like that. Either that, or else drink doesn't sit well with Saju. Some men are like that. One beer and they turn into a different animal. Some are like dogs and some are like wild pigs. Saju looks like one anyway.

I had said that aloud once. It was before she was married. I was trying to warn her. The way he looks, I said, he'll run to fat very quickly. Running a cafe, it is guaranteed. He will grow breasts inside his shirt. Wait and see, I told her.

It was not a wise thing to say. The thing that makes a girl run after unsuitable boys is the opposition of her elders. It adds fuel to the fire. Where else can a girl display the iron of her spirit? The only thing she can choose is who to love. And frankly, she didn't choose too badly. Saju has a bit of land on his mother's side. An only son. He'll inherit. His father has bought him the cafe. He's doing all right. And he shows respect. Not from our caste, but okay. At least, he's not a plantation worker. I've known girls who are such idiots. Just this last week, the Ladies Club secretary came over. Bursting with gossip! She was so excited, her face was red. She was not smiling, of course. One can't smile about these things. But I could see that she was happy deep inside her belly, the way her eyes were shining. She knew who it was, but of course, she had to pretend. She did not take the girl's name, but almost everything else, she told me.

A chit of a girl, just in the tenth standard. Imagine? A girl from one of the biggest estates. Same school as both our girls. Caught loitering in the school building on a Sunday morning. Not wearing her uniform either. They say she was discovered in an empty classroom with a boy. Thankfully, not in a compromising position. She was just showing him around the school, the girl claims. Turns out, he's a worker on the plantation. The boy couldn't even spell out his own name. Totally illiterate.

These girls! Brainless. It's not even like she was out with a boy of her own age. He is three years older. Almost a man. Eighteen years old, they're saying. Of course, with these people, you can never be sure. No birth certificate, no school ID. He could have been twenty years old, what do we know?

I began to tell Devaki about the scandal. Knowing her, she would be sympathetic to the girl. Besides, the school is her alma mater. Still. I had thought, after marriage, she would have grown some brains. But, high hopes.

No birth certificate means he could also be seventeen. Or sixteen. She's fifteen. Say, he's sixteen. He's never been to school. She takes him to see her school. Wasn't that a good thing? She rose above four different types of prejudice, didn't she?

Phish! I had told Vinny years ago, it's pure luck that Devaki didn't pick that other friend of hers. It could easily have been him instead. Long phone calls, talking and walking. Books being exchanged. Poetry books, with those flimsy pink and yellow covers. Those book covers always reminded me of the walls of certain lower middle-class drawing rooms. It's a peculiar shade of pink and yellow and pistachio green.

Imagine, what if it was the other boy? That's what I said when Appa was storming around the house threatening to beat Devaki.

Not that she cried. No begging, no weeping. Wisp of a girl, but the way she held herself! Even I used to be afraid of Appa. Why deny it? But Devaki? The way she was back then, I was a little afraid of her too. The last few days before her wedding, she would spend the whole afternoon standing at the kitchen door, at the back. Cleaning out each bristle of her hairbrush. Combing out each shiny strand of her hair. She would file her nails. Polish her leather shoes. The whole day she just waited on herself, hand and foot. Like she was a princess living alone in some ivory tower.

Phish! Marriage is such a thing. It knocks the steel out of a woman's spine. Look at her now. Twisting her fingers around her saree. Now her father is thick with her husband, she's done for. Where will she escape to?

I sat her down in the kitchen before preparing the evening's dessert. I had to hold her hands to make her stop fidgeting. She kept picking up a spoon, a plate, a basket, putting it back in the wrong place. I made her sit in the chair and chatted about normal things. Both my girls are playing hockey now, but the older one plays better. I asked her to come to their school's sports day event. Told her about the guests in our cottages. Tourists are a pain nowadays. They want to hang around the kitchen and chit-chat all the time. Can't they just eat breakfast and get out? Look around the town, find some elephant or tiger or whatever for entertainment.

Oh dear lord, the photography! Twenty-four hours, they're at it. They get up, brush their teeth and they have to take a photo of their face in the mirror. Ant, bee, spoon, plate, donkey, car, leaf, moon. Grown-ups, mind you! They look at normal things and point a camera at it. *Oh, look at that leaf! Oh, that moon!*

As if they've come here from outer space and their moon was square instead of round. They're like toddlers.

What do they want? Attention. Someone! Look at me. Someone! Touch me. Daily requests for massage. They'll pay for it, fine. But where do I find the labour? Mariam will not leave her house job. She comes in for just two hours a day. Then these people get sulky if you say, sorry, no massage lady is available.

All these little problems, I was telling Devaki. Then it came down. Drip, drip, drip. Down her face. And still, she would not say a word.

I took her in my arms. I kept calling her Baby. I said, Baby, talk to him, talk like a friend. He was your boyfriend, after all. More tears. She kept shaking her head.

I took her to my own bedroom and scolded her for having made such a mess of her hair. It used to be so thick and glossy, now look at it! Birds do better with their nests. I combed it out, rubbed in some jasmine oil, made a nice knot at the nape of her neck. Pinned a flower on one side. That's how her Amma used to wear her hair. I took a picture of her and sent it to her phone. See, you look just like Amma, I said. That set her off again. Drip, drip, drip.

I said, Baby. See here. The nature of desire is very tricky. Delicate, like a butterfly's wing. Love always catches you unawares. It's like being out by the lake, seeing a ripple in the water, and perhaps the sun glints in a particular way and a tiny fish leaps up in that moment when your eye is unprepared for it. It captivates you. But the same water, the same ripple, the same sun, and the same fish may not touch your heart on another day. Love is that landscape. If someone points to a beautiful picture and says, look! So much beauty! You see the beauty but you cannot feel it. Your heart is not warmed by it. But when nobody is asking you to observe, then you may suddenly feel it. On its own, it comes. Do you understand?

She had stopped crying by now. Suddenly, she caught my hand in hers and put it on top of her head.

Don't let them burn me.

I swear, it was as if winter had arrived a month early. I shivered. I asked, What? Why? Is it about money? She shook her head, No.

Bury me, that's all. I don't want to be burnt. Remember how Amma stood up for our grandmother's last wish? She made Appa bury her body. I'm asking you for a promise. Will you do that much for me?

I prised my hand free. Baby, you have a husband now. You tell him. Next to him, Appa is here to make decisions. You can make a will if you are so troubled. But why worry about burial and burning now? You have a long life ahead.

After that, she said nothing. She left without eating lunch.

I know what to do. I'll send Mariam over to her place.

Prelude to a Riot

She's good with her hands and we have no bookings for tomorrow.

We must also give her some of her gold. Maybe on her birthday. We never gave her anything at the wedding. Amma, as long as she was alive, had kept a box full of jewellery for her. She is an only daughter, after all. I don't want a dead woman's curse on my head.

I noticed the way Devaki was looking at my bracelets. Her mouth opened, like she was about to say something but stopped herself. Who can blame her? Saju keeps her well. She dresses neatly. Had a bit of gold in her ears. Still. A woman needs gold that's her own. Something that has not been bought by the husband.

Look at Mariam's case. Her people had nothing to give, not even a gold chain. Zero proposals. If it weren't for the magic of her hands, she would have been cooking, or worse, breaking stones on the road until she keeled over and died. One gold chain and it would have been a totally different story.

What a pity, she will not work here full-time. So many times I have said, Mariam, think about it. A proper salary plus tips. You can even spend the night here in the house. I said, I'll double the money anyone else is giving you. Plus hot meals. But she's another donkey. Obstinate mule of a woman.

Can't depend on anyone these days. Take Mariam.

Annie Zaidi

Nice enough but no guarantee that she will stick around. These days her nose is a little higher than it used to be. She's been pawing around with that Royal Bakery fellow. She will not tell me, of course, but don't I know why she needs her afternoons free? Nights are difficult, because he is a married man. I asked her indirectly, everything okay? Any problem at home?

Damned if she will tell. Clams up at once. She will not take the man's name. But just mention Royal Bakery and then watch her eyes. Ah, that great liquid hope!

Well, she is allowed to hope. Maybe he will take her as a wife after all. These people are allowed. Second, third, fourth. Once she is the wife of a bakery owner, she won't be coming around to thump and knead the naked bodies of tourist ladies, will she?

Phish! What a hunger they have to be touched! Give them a whole hour but the whining never stops. *Don't you offer a ninety-minute package? Don't you do chocolate wraps?*

I know what to do. I will send Mariam over to Devaki's house tomorrow, and along with Mariam, I'll send a puppy from Shuku's litter. Put it in a nice basket with a ribbon. Should I send two?

No. Two will be too much for her to handle. I should send the male. With girls, there are problems. They grow up and next thing, you have six new puppies. Devaki doesn't even have a shed outside her house. Or, who

63

knows? Maybe I can send two puppies, male and female. Let her have her own litter of six.

She used to like puppies. That first litter, we had four puppies, all of them looked exactly like Shuku. God! The way she cried when Appa sold them off! Not in front of us, though. Devaki never cried like that. She used to go into the shed and cry with her arms around Shuku. Mad girl.

These four are probably Shuku's last litter. Two of her pups died last week under Vinny's jeep. Fifteen hundred times I've told him, look properly when you reverse. The puppies are playing around the shed. Careless, this man of mine. He did the same thing, twice. The first time, he didn't even realize what had happened. Mariam saw the puppy lying dead and she told me. But I didn't want to go out to look at it. I said, you take it away and bury it somewhere. Or call one of the cleaning maids. I can't spoil my mood, not when I'm cooking. When I see or hear disturbing things, it somehow gets into the food. The flavour is always off. That's what happened with the second puppy.

I couldn't avoid going out that day. The little pup yelped so loudly and Shuku set up such a fantastic barking that I had to peep outside, and there it was. Mouth open. Phish! I wanted to cry. Vinny had stopped the jeep a few yards ahead. He was shouting, dammit! Dammit! Then he called one of the men to pick it up and bury it. I swear, sometimes I think this estate is one giant graveyard. Five dogs were already buried near the gates. Here and there, there must be birds and squirrels. Devaki always insisted on burying any animal she found lying dead.

Four puppies were too many for us anyway. Plus, the racket. We can't keep any more. Two dogs are fine to keep. What does it cost to feed them? Offal, goat, pig, nothing these dogs won't eat. Appa says he wants more dogs on the estate. But I think I'll give one to Devaki and one to the secretary of the Ladies Club. I don't like her face but she comes over so often and she always says 'nice-nice' to everything I make. One has to keep up these things. Give and take. Not that she really wants a 65 dog. She just wants more gossip.

What gossip can I offer? These damn tourists are married and boring. They want to know if the same pots are used to cook vegetables and meat. I swear, one of these days I'll put up a big sign in the dining room: *Same pots, same spoons, same plates, same cook!*

What is your life, Bavna, eh? Six cottages, boring tourists. Forty years old. You will be doing this for another twenty years. Who else will do it? Vinny, two girls, Appa, dogs, homestay. That's it. Phish! Better not think too much.

Devaki had said something once. It must have been

before Amma died. She had called on the landline. Appa wasn't talking to her at that time. She wanted to speak with her mother but it was I who picked up the phone. I heard 'hello' and knew it was her. Then, just silence. I said, Baby? Is it you? You can always come home if you like. Appa is out for the whole day. She just repeated that word. *Home.*

They say home is where your heart is.

I was irritated. Was her drama not over yet? She had got her way, had she not? Why prolong the drama? But then she said something else.

Home is that place you can never leave. No?

The Self-Respect Forum Sends a Letter to the Editor

Subject: The publishing of a poem referencing the Goddess's waist

Dear Sir,

This is with respect to the poem published in your otherwise esteemed publication, dated xx/xx/xxxx, on the lower half of the fourth page.

The poem occupied a box equal to three column widths and at least six inches long. Firstly, the forum feels strongly that this much space need not be devoted to cultural inputs, especially on weekdays. This is the only esteemed publication which is owned by a local person and devoted mainly to local news. There are only eight pages on weekdays and the decision to allocate so much space to poems is not understood by us.

Our strong complaint must be registered particularly against the poem which was printed on the aforementioned date. It is written with mischievous intent. The first line itself suggests a religious overtone:

Mother, but not just mine

Clearly, this is a reference to the Mother Goddess and we find it very troubling that it should be published at a time when the festival of the Goddess is around the corner.

The fourth and fifth lines are very peculiar. As such, we feel they barely mask the writer's mischievous intent, which we can nevertheless discern.

Whither breasts, milky brown?
Withered breasts, walnut brown

We are aware that mothers give milk to small children but this description appears to insult the source of nourishment.

The worst offending lines are the fourteenth, fifteenth, sixteenth and seventeenth.

Finger of him who is no god (no, don't apologize for him)
traced his own coat of arms upon your waist.
You kept his brand in the shape of a son
and he set you afloat when he was done.

Annie Zaidi

Sir, there is little doubt as to the intent of the writer. He has referenced the Goddess indirectly. There is a reference to a 'god' and also to the immersion of the Goddess in water. However, no man may brand the Goddess. The reference to a coat of arms is clearly a foreign mishmash which has come on account of English-medium education, which has sadly confused our people.

This is a clearly vulgar way of looking at the figure of the Mother, even if she were not the Goddess, as she is indicated.

We urge the editor to take stringent action and stop publishing material by this author, 'DeeD'. It is evident that he wishes to cause mischief, otherwise DeeD is no real name. We are also noting an odd trend of this paper publishing no-name poets. There have been two poems from ABC in the last two months. This is the third one by DeeD. Please use real names.

We demand an apology from this publication as well as from the writer.

As undersigned
Self-Respect Forum members

The Editor Responds on the Op-Ed Page

Editor's View: Self-Respect Forum's complaint about a poem referencing DeeD's mother

Dear Sirs,

I trust that I am accurately addressing you as Sirs, for I noticed that all the signatories from the Self-Respect Forum have appended 'Mr' in front of their names. I also noticed that you have addressed me as 'Sir'. Perhaps you have failed to note that for the last eleven years, the editor of your esteemed local publication is a female.

You have also presumed that DeeD is a 'he'. It is the opinion of our consulting literary editor that there is a likelihood that DeeD is a woman since feminine themes dominate her work, and also because while writing of the female body, the voice seems to emerge from inside it. Thus, the amorous gaze is effectively neutered. The word neutered is not mine but has been suggested by the literary editor, a man, who agrees that DeeD is talented, whether male or female, or transgender, and that their expression should be encouraged. Praise has come in from other literary quarters.

We have made no attempt to trace the identities of DeeD and ABC. They send poems via post and have not collected the honorarium, pitiful as the amount is, which we offer to all the poets we publish. It is rare in today's world, to seek neither money nor credit. Even the pseudonyms are vague, which might prevent them from creating a distinct literary identity, like many poets do before owning up to their pseudonyms later in life.

Your complaint has been considered by an internal panel comprising disinterested parties. None of us feels that the mother in the poem (a) refers to the Goddess, (b) is disrespectful to either mothers or goddesses, (c) refers to idol immersion.

Your grief about the perils of an English education may be well founded. Certainly, your letter is one of the fallouts of an English education. The British did not quite understand our faith, having lost touch with their own pagan deities. They were fascinated by it though, and we must thank their scholars and translators with all our heart, for they preserved, documented and restored to us much that was in danger of being lost.

The trouble with the British was not just their fear of 'savage' or 'native' culture, which was a complex, syncretic, and always shifting form. They wanted to grasp it rather than flow with it. They were scared of a river-like flow of culture and ideas, since they were uprooted themselves and desperately needed to hold on to the familiar. Sometimes I believe that this is the colonizer's true legacy: an inability to look at other humans as being capable of, and deserving of, fluidity—to flow as free as a river while simultaneously being as self-possessed as the ocean.

We must not forget that anybody who seeks to block the flow of ideas, or people, creates artificial hurricanes.

As for breasts, our goddesses have been bare-chested for millennia. The waists of goddesses have often been touched by gods, who take mortal form. This is evidenced by our ancient art and, indeed, ancient art is our only tangible article of faith. If not for art, how would we know all that we think we know?

I would urge Self-Respect Forum members to make a trip to our local museum this very weekend. It stands woefully neglected. There are no notes of explanation. Our civilization's giant leap towards technology is nowhere in evidence. The state seems to be of the view that ancient culture must be preserved through the most ancient devices available to mankind. Still, there are statues of goddesses, yakshis, and mortal women. The beauty and delicacy of craftsmanship will restore your spirits. You may also discover some of the motifs that have inspired a new poem by DeeD (see facing page).

Besides, the garden outside the museum is ideal for picnics in this weather. Do take your wives and children along. Do not cut them off from their roots. Else, what is the difference between the cultural imperialism of which we accuse Western nations, and ourselves?

Those of you who are interested in poetry and our ancient literary traditions may be interested in attending a one-day seminar (fee nominal, covers lunch and tea) that will be held next week at the University, helmed by a celebrated scholar. It is a unique opportunity.

The Editor

New Poem by DeeD

Surrender
was not a word one came upon in ancient texts describing
war which

Is inevitable
for surely, there were kings who bowed their heads and
perhaps breathed

Easier
knowing, there was no longer a need to stockpile industrial
quantities of testosterone.

Said
one such king to me: I pay tribute but so what? My
one-fourth feeds a king more pitiful

Than
I, who lolls on velvet thrones cushioned by the three-
fourth that is still mine and Lo! I am

Done
with all battle. Come, girls! Come feel this silken doublet.
Come into my paisley arms.
@DeeD

Prelude to a Riot

Garuda Answers a Question by Posing a Question

Why did the Mughals invade so much? Good question. Thank you for asking, Shiv.

How do kingdoms expand? The land is not elastic. It's not like blowing air into a balloon. Consider this sentence in your books. *At the height of its power, the Maratha kingdom stretched—* Anyone?

Panipat to Mangalore! Very nice, Deepika. Let's modify that, since political maps do not come in neat squares or circles. Look at this map. We could say it extended as far north as Panipat and a bit beyond, cutting into Punjab, down to Mangalore along the southwest, across to the east. Some territories came directly under their control. Present-day Gujarat, Madhya Pradesh. Tanjore. How did this empire expand?

Armies are sent out. Armies fight. Sometimes the more powerful king offers a no-war option to the other guy—pay me and keep your behind attached to the throne. This is called paying tribute. The other king reacts, depending on whether he has confidence in his own army. Sometimes, he just has a big ego and he is beaten and driven out.

There can also be a peace treaty. The winning side would dictate terms, make allies for future wars. But still, land is finite. Expansion for one translates into shrinking for another. Maurya suffered when Shunga got ambitious. Lodi suffered when Babur got ambitious. Mughal empire shrank, Maratha grew. Down south, Vijayanagar grew at the expense of Arcot, Madurai. Take Bengaluru. The Marathas sold it for the princely sum of three lakh rupees.

No, don't laugh. Three lakhs *was* a princely sum. The Mughals could claim it as part of their empire. But who had real control? The Wodeyar. The Wodeyars ruled from Mysore. From roughly the fifteenth century up to India's independence. Except for the Hyder-Tipu years.

Mysore used to be a small kingdom once, under the Vijayanagar empire. But power is a shifty thing. Vijayanagar grew weak. The Wodeyars saw an opportunity. Mysore had an alliance with—? Any guesses?

No, not the Cholas. Seventeenth-century Mysore had an alliance with the Mughals. Emperor Aurangzeb had granted the Mysore king a nice title: Jug Deo Raj. King of the World. Of course 'world' does not include Delhi. Haha!

That pen is not a lollipop, Shiv, don't suck on it like that.

Your father has told you everything about Mysore, eh? So what was the name of the King of the World, not including Delhi?

Chikka Devaraja, correct. And what did he do?

He expanded his kingdom. An expensive undertaking. So? He had to raise taxes. Soldiers have to be paid. Farmers, they were called ryots, felt they were paying too much. They started to rebel. Some of the priests were supporting the farmers. But without taxes, how can a king realize his ambitions? So the rebellion was quashed. How many of you have heard of the Jangama Massacre? One hand, two hands, three hands... I'm impressed! Who knew?

Four hundred priests were killed. So it is said. There is no official record from that era. But then, why would any king officially document his own excesses? Some people say it is oral history. Some say it is just a legend. But if a ruler sanctions a massacre, they don't put it into his official biography. In those days, they didn't publish unauthorized biographies. No human rights commissions either.

Does that partially address your doubts, Shiv? That question which you were trying to ask, without quite asking? Yes?

Strange! I can hear the fan whirring today. Either the fan is working very hard or 10-B has gone very quiet.

Vinny's Soliloquy

The men, their backs are odd. Have you noticed? Like the spine is trying to jump out of the skin.

Bavna? Sleeping?

Ten, ten-fifteen, she's out. Out like a light. She won't talk to our guests. Dinner is at seven, washing up at eight-thirty, and she's in bed by nine-thirty. When she makes sweet dishes, I keep telling her, serve them a bit later. Guests can relish sweets better if they are served later at night. Give them time. One drink, two drinks. Let the dinner settle down nicely. What's the hurry? And how does she talk to me?

You get yourself another wife. One more wife for duty after ten o'clock. From six in the morning to ten at night,

I am here.

Ha! I also say, fine. I'll get another wife. But she's also a bold one. Haha!

Please. I am the one asking. You bring another woman home, if someone will agree. Or you can convert. You bring three. No problem. I need three more people to help manage this place.

Mad creature, my Bavna. More hands are needed, that much is true. These people, the men are okay for plantation work, but not inside the house. Cannot allow that. That fellow, Mommad. Just see his face! He looks like he has run away from jail. That scar on his nose.

Mommad. His body is something else. He looks like he is carved out of black wood. His back is also funny, with the spine popping out of his skin. But no doubt, strong fellow. The way he got the jeep out of the mud? Oof!

The path to the south gate is horrible. Appa says, raise it. *Use them. These people can do it. They can do everything. Road work, construction, rice fields, plantation work. Bomb work. They pick it up fast.*

Appa was laughing when he said it. We were all down at the bar. Not serious like. Everyone was laughing. Kadir was there too. Appa said they can do anything, bombs or anything! Kadir started laughing. The way he laughs, with his big stomach shaking. But then, when he thought nobody was looking at him, his face suddenly

81

changed. I was watching his face in one of the mirrors on the walls of the bar.

Bomb making is not rocket science. Anybody can do it. But these people, they have one advantage. They are good at doing things with their hands. All that tailoring and wood carving and silver filigree work. See the ironwork they did for our estate gates. Black magic. That's what Amma used to say when she saw them doing it. The kind of work they can do, our people can never match it. Their fingers have a special something. Saju says they send little boys to work on carpets. Tight little knots with tiny fingers. Very expensive carpets. Making money all over the world. Brassy fellows.

Bold. Brassy. This much I'll say about them, they are not afraid of a challenge. Like that afternoon when the jeep got stuck near the banana grove. I gave the engine full power but there was too much sludge. Then I looked around. Mommad was working nearby. I called out to him. Didn't remember his name. I just said, Ey! Waved him over.

He came and he stared at the mud and the wheel. Just looked at it for a long time. I thought he would call his people, then together they would pull and push and somehow I'd manage to get the wheel free. But this fellow? He just knots his lungi tighter, brings four-five rocks.

Start the engine, sir.

Annie Zaidi

His hands under the wheel, shoulder against the wheel. His feet clawing into the mud. One, two, three and hup! Oof! I'll never forget that day. And you see his waist? Like a teenage girl's.

These people, they can break their backs and still stand upright. They're made of some different stuff. Must be genetic. Just think about it. Fifty, sixty people. They came here without a single blanket between them. Before they came, I had to pay at least one hundred local workers in the planting season. Now these sixty people do the same work, in the same time. And I pay less. Why should I pay more?

The contractor told me, these are great workers. But there is only one condition. This group is from one village and they will work together on one estate. Whole clan has landed up here. They brought their women. Children too. Nobody eats a meal without having earned it. Every single man, woman, child will be put to work. Babies are rolling naked in the mud.

That way, these people cannot be changed. Didn't Bavna try? She made an offer.

Send the children to us. They can do small jobs, like carrying dishes into the dining hall. They can keep the tips.

Stubborn people. They said no. They like to keep their children close. Huh! We are going to eat up their children or what?

Prelude to a Riot

Anyway. Better for us. Their children would have disturbed my guests. Or they would give competition to the dogs. These tourists are always feeding cheap glucose biscuits to the dogs. I had to stop one fellow today. Sorry, no, I said. Buy good dog biscuits if you want to feed my dogs. Glucose biscuits are okay for the strays.

Sly fellow, Mommad. What does he say to me? *We thank God for bringing us here. The air is good. And if there's any difficulty, you are there. We will come straight to you.*

Huhuhuhuh! God has brought them here, it seems. The bloody contractor brought them and he kept twenty per cent of the full season's wages for himself. Idiot. God has brought him! Ha!

84

Yes, he will talk of the sweet air, won't he? First, they were living in plastic shacks on the highway. Now I am seeing huts made of straw, wood, scrap-iron. Banana leaves for thatching the roof. They keep sneaking a little bit from here and there. Otherwise, where do they get bamboo? The rates of wood in the market are touching the sky. Would anyone give it to them free? Even banana leaves. Who gives them that? God?

Huh! Sly people. Saju was telling me, his mother's farm has a tree which is ready for felling. I told him, wait. Let me find one of our regular fellows to come and chop it. Don't ask one of them. They'll always set aside a bit for themselves. Especially this wood business, you can't trust them. They're fully into wood, so they'll always steal a little bit and make money on the side. Must take it up with the Self-Respect Forum. We must keep the field labourers out of the wood business.

The meeting is at ten tomorrow morning. I told Bavna, why don't you take an interest? The way she snapped at me!

Will you cook and supervise the maids? Make sure bed sheets are changed in all six cottages and feed the girls and the dogs? You start doing that. Then I'll see about taking an interest in the forum.

Anyway. The Forum is full of idiots. Lazy bums. But they're better than the guys in the Farmers Association. On the phone, everyone says yesyesyes, notgood, notgood. But can you get them to commit to any action?

Appa wrote a letter to the district magistrate. Nice, polite letter. Just to warn the administration about infiltration. Keep a check on strangers in town. Isn't that our duty? Security is a collective responsibility. Don't they keep announcing it at the railway station?

But how many signed the letter? Three! Three out of thirty-nine members in our unit of the Farmers Association. Even Timmy would not sign. I had a word with Bavna's brothers. After that, we managed to get at least five signatures and Appa sent it off.

I was saying, no, let's wait. Let us go and meet other elders. But Appa stood firm.

I will send it with five signatures. Next time, we will have the support of minimum fifteen. You wait and see. After this, we will get our Self-Respect Forum to sign one more letter. Next time, we will mention the martyr's memorial at the association meeting. They will have to sign a petition for that at least, or they will drown in shame. After that, I'll bring up this problem of outsiders. Those without documents should not be hired. We'll pass a resolution.

I wanted to ask Appa, what will happen if the resolution fails? But then, I thought, why ask all these questions? Appa's head, it heats up too fast. Always was like that.

Still. Appa's got his own style. He somehow gets things done. He got the state unit of the SRF to come here and do a public event. Now the state president has sent a letter of support, backing our demand for a new martyr's memorial.

For this sort of work, Appa has full energy. He never could work the land. Amma used to say, it is better that he remains busy with outside matters and does not ruin her crop.

They forgot to mix earth in his milk. That's what she used to say. She made me sit with her when she did the accounts. She said, don't depend on his help after I'm gone. Funny. The way she left us, suddenly. Woke up fine in the morning. By afternoon, she was gone.

She used to say it. *I'll go easy. You worry about yourselves.*

Two big fellows from the secretariat had come down to pay their condolences. The priests also came on their own. I didn't have to go out to call anyone when she died. Big funeral. Cost us, though. Feeding all those who came to condole.

The local labour market has been spoilt rotten. The way the state pampers these tribals. Poverty card, old-age pension card. Rice, twenty-five kilos free! Or is it thirty-five? Free sugar. Kerosene. Free school. Their children get free lunch in school. Now if these people grace our estate with their presence, we are supposed to be grateful.

The state, huh? Our money. And it's not like the tribes are local as such. Appa had traced it out on a map once. Their ancestors came from the hills, south and west of here. They keep moving through the forests. They admit to that. So how can anyone say that they are the original inhabitants of the land? What is the meaning of indigenous if you don't even stay in one place?

Humph! That way, why should we not be called indigenous? We are a tribe, too. Fine, we have farmland and all. So what? Just because they live in the forests, they think they can blackmail us by refusing to work for the old rate.

Prelude to a Riot

Appa says we were the original inhabitants of the land. Not these tribes who live in the forest. Nonono. They came from across the hills, which means they crossed the state border, and who knows their origins? Appa says we didn't go looking for them in the forest. They came and asked for work on our estates. So? No problem. Fine. Working is all right. But this land, the hills, valleys, all of it belonged to us. All of it! Slowly, or perhaps not so slowly, we have been reduced to scraping a living off of one acre here and three acres there. These outsiders, is anyone keeping a count of them? Does anyone calculate how much they've taken?

But Appa has been keeping track. Every acre an outsider buys, he puts it in his notebook. At the Self-Respect Forum's annual march, we are going to present the numbers to the general body. Shake them out of their stupor. Give it one more season, Appa says. Then these forest tribes will come back to work.

You'll see. And they'll take less money too! Their noses have gone up high in the air after the government started spoiling them. You watch. First, these outsiders have to be reminded what's what.

These people can take the rate we are offering or they can go to hell. No lack of farm workers in this country. There's been a drought up north. The labour contractor was telling me, he is bringing in more people from the east. They'll work for even less. The women will accept a rate one-third less than the men, he says.

Tricky thing. Drought. But not here. The rains have been okay this time.

Look at her. Sleeping on. No worries. I tell Bavna, get a safety deposit box. See? Gold bangles are just lying on top of the dressing table. No locks. I keep telling her, be careful. But she is another crazy type. Not a care in the world. Just lies down on the bed and falls asleep.

She was telling me the other day, alcohol interferes with sleep. I said, what alcohol? Beer? Beer is not alcohol. It's just a cold drink. I can drive fine with a bottle of beer in one hand and drinking with my face turned up to the sky. I don't even look at the road. Steady hand, steady feet. Beer is just froth. You should also drink a bit, I tell Bavna. Two beers and you'll feel lighter.

I can see that. So light, you are floating among the treetops. But you have to come down to ground level before you can fall asleep.

Woman has gone mad. She used to drink with me. When we got married, we'd have one drink at night. Appa, me and her. Only Amma did not drink. Devaki was too young, of course, not even married. Saju drinks well. Keeps up with us. Beer doesn't hurt. I told him, you should get her to drink a little. It will keep her calm. Bavna stopped because of the babies. Now she drinks

89

milk at night like a baby herself. Haha!

Wait till the girls grow up. Hahahaha! They'll ask for a taste of beer soon. Then we'll see if she still prefers to drink milk like a baby.

Fast asleep. No worries. What is her difficulty in life? She just has to decide whether to cook mutton curry with coconut, or without. For me, it is about action. Have to sort people out.

Damn Mommad. Six men I asked for, for Timmy's estate. Just for a week, two weeks. Mommad starts bargaining. Wants me to promise they'll get extra money for the bus tickets, and lunch at the other estate so the boys are not going hungry. What next? I should chauffeur them to and fro in my jeep? And now, this new mess.

Should have picked the men out myself. Eh, never mind. We'll fix it. But Bavna is right. No unnecessary drama.

Think of the girl's family. And we're in the middle of harvest season.

Sensible woman, Bavna. Can't have them running off. Not in harvest season. But we'll fix it. Soon.

Mommad's Soliloquy

Hero! Ack-thoo!

Old lion is in town! Ho! What madness came upon me! I ran all the way back after seeing the poster in town. Calling out to this one and that one. Uncle! Son!

My wife's eyes, smiling. All those dialogues I used to whisper in her ears in the evenings were from his films. She knows what it means to me. Old lion is in town! Oh, the noise I made.

My mother had thrashed me because of this man. I used to steal two rupees every day to watch his films on the screen.

Sitting on a mat with rocks poking your arse, for that you want two rupees?

My mother would scold and twist my ears. Once she had even placed a burning coal on my palm as punishment for stealing. But I kept doing it, until she put her head on my shoulder and wept.

The same damn story. How many times will you steal for the same thing? Seven times you've been. Watch it from a distance, can't you?

So then I began climbing a tree to watch the film one more time, this time for free. Lying flat on my belly so that the tent-man could not count my head in the dark. The things I used to do to watch this man in action. Madness!

Who cared about the story? It was always the same story. The hero was strong, so what if he was poor? Or, he was rich but he was unhappy despite all his wealth. He would fight twenty men. He would love a good girl, so what if she was poor? Or, a rich girl would love him. He would spout dialogues that inflamed your tongue. Like bad liquor.

What dialogues! The words he spoke on screen would open up all the wounds of one's heart, and then sew them back. Those words were like alcohol rubbed on your wounds. It would sting, but it would also clean your heart. And, sometimes, they were like rose water on the eyes. Or like meat. Fleshy, juicy, full of the power of marrow. You felt those words go down smooth and sit inside the hollows of your bones.

I could die for those words, steal for the man who gave those words tongue. My fists entered his fists when he picked himself up from the dust, blood trickling down the side of his mouth. His kicks entered my sleep. How I kicked about at night after I'd been to a night show!

Now he was coming to town. My hero. I would see him, for free, at the rally. His face was on all the posters. Older, true. But not too old. The photo is at least ten years old, I could guess. It's from the time when he was doing all those punching-kicking films. Then he became the heroine's father. Who wants to watch fathers trying to be funny? I once spent five rupees on one of his later films, but never again.

Still. To see the real man, the thought set me on fire. I went around saying to everyone, let's go. Let's all go.

Fool. Fool, fool, fool! I said, forget the day's wage. We'll all go to the rally. The boss will understand. Can't we go to a rally too? It's open. The public is invited. It said so on the poster.

I pleaded with my people. It's right here. One hour, if we walk. Twenty minutes in the bus. I said to my wife, you at least must come with me. How about it? Me and you. He will get up on the stage and he'll say his best dialogues. Then I'll say those lines with him. You clap for me. The public will clap for him.

Prelude to a Riot

Small mercies. God has given her more sense than He gave me. She said, no. There's too much work here. But you go, she said. So I went, alone. The only fool in the family who actually went.

He didn't say a single memorable line from his films. He made a speech like a bloody leader. The poster had other faces on it, all leaders from this state. I don't know their names. They all spoke, one by one. For one bloody hour, they filled the crap pit of our ears. They said, he has come for you all. To meet people, greet people.

Fool, fool, fool! I didn't even know that he had become a leader. He will be standing for elections. Getting mixed up with all this. Fool! I never spent two rupees on a newspaper. Spent it all watching this man turn into a hero. And what does he have to say?

At first he just sat on stage, hiding behind black glasses. Then he stands up. His hands are held high, first right, then left. Waving at the public. Joining his hands above his head, bowing to the public. Meanwhile, the other leader had blood in his eyes. He was on the boil.

Those who do not like the way things are done here, they can leave. They can go where they are welcome. And if they are not welcome anywhere, then they can walk into the sea. Else, you live here quietly. And die quietly too. If they believe in returning to the earth, they should be prepared to turn into manure for our fields. Why take up space even

Annie Zaidi

after death? Can anyone escape death by putting up a stone and writing one's name on it? Let me assure them, they will not escape!

People clapped. On my right, on my left, clapping hands. My hero, sitting up there, showing his teeth. Not getting up the way he had in *Angel of Death*, and knocking out the villain's teeth. Now he is not breaking the villain's greasy jaw. He is sitting behind the villain in his starchy new clothes. Garlands of roses around his neck.

At last it was his turn to speak. When they called him to the mic, the crowd sent up such a thunder, it made the hair on my neck rise. He stood up. He said he was beholden to the other leaders for giving him a chance to serve the people. The leaders showed their teeth.

I could not hear the rest of it. I was sitting on the ground, looking up at his thick figure, his too white clothes. Then I began to speak his best lines myself.

Yes, it runs in the gutters of the city but our blood is still blood.

You can try touching me, boss. But then, I will touch you too. And your touch may be a hammer coming down on my back but my touch will be a ton of bricks coming down on your head.

It isn't tears, sweetheart. It's just the rain. Sometimes, this is the way the rain comes down.

This one drop of sweat, Daddy, this one drop is worth

more than your fancy suits. Your palace. Your factories. One drop of salt and water.

Am I less of a man? Let me show you! This is red blood. Look! What colour is it? Is it green? It is black? Is yours any different? Is yours milky white?... Come here. Your blood, my blood, let it mix.

Our blood is the ink with which history will be written.

I don't have a name. I had no mother, no father who would give me a name. So you can give me a new name. Say anything at all. Whatever sound soothes your lips. I will accept whatever passes your lips as my name.

How many names a hero takes on! A hundred different names. In one of his films, he had my name. Mohammad. After watching that film, I etched the name on my arm. Got it tattooed. It was my name, but it was restored to me through him. And now? I look at the tattoo and I wonder. Is my name still my own, or has he taken even that from me?

I left the rally and wandered around town for the rest of the day. I hadn't looked at this town properly, although we've been here for months. On the plantations, it's just work, dawn to dusk.

I saw the big school building, the one with a white cross outside. Opposite, there is another school for very small children. They wear little red shorts, both the girls and the boys. I moved away from the gates quickly, before

I could start thinking impossible things. It is too late for me to dream. Both my children are too big for the little children's school.

Bus stop. Cinema. Hotels. Bakeries. I ate a wonderful new thing. A flaky, baked roti that was stuffed with coconut and sugar, and some other things that I do not know the names of. I sat eating it in the sunshine, on the steps of the mosque. Then I went in to wash my hands at the tap. There were other men inside, all washing up for prayers.

How long since? I've forgotten how to wash up for prayers. They had taught me. Only once in my life did I have the time to learn anything. I was eight or nine. My mother sent me to learn how to read and write at the mosque. I was already stealing for the cinema, but she hoped I could be salvaged. They did teach me to pray in the few days that I showed up. After one month, my mother had to pull me out of the classes. Harvest season. She needed an extra pair of hands. Never stopped needing hands. Fields, buildings. We were always on the move.

I felt ashamed to have forgotten how to wash for the prayers. Three times face, hands, feet, nose, this much I remember, but was there a sequence to be followed? I waited until the other men had gone indoors. Then I washed my hands, face, feet. One has to be clean, that is the main thing. And to accept one's own intention.

Prelude to a Riot

The mosque was cool and dark. It smelt damp, like when rain gets trapped inside the walls. I looked about. The men were all facing away from me but I felt as if they were aware that I was standing behind them and not saying my prayers. So I crept out again.

An old man stood outside holding a steel box. Resting against the wall was a piece of cardboard on which something was written. I told him I couldn't read. He looked at me for a long moment, then he read it out aloud. The new mosque needs tiles and wooden frames and doors. Anyone can contribute anything.

I said I could spare only five rupees. He asked me to put it in the box. The coin landed with a dull thunk.

Your five is equal to five thousand.

The old man shook the box, like a happy child shaking a gullak. There were no other coins in the box, I could guess. My lone coin moved lustily between paper notes.

I opened my mouth to speak but it was like all the words I knew had been sucked out of my belly. I felt utterly empty, and filled with bubbles of light.

I started to leave then, but I don't know what got into me. I asked, what if I made the tiles? We, me and my nephew, we can do it. My nephew has done glazed tile work before. He did it for two years in a factory. He can create colourful patterns on clay tiles. You just have to help us with tools. He can copy designs on metal if

98

you draw them on paper. How about it? I will ask Majju. He's a good boy. Still growing. Teach him good things. We couldn't send him to school. But it's not too late, is it? You'll see. Majju's hands have a beautiful, light touch. He can paint walls too. Doors, windows, gates, grilles. I would rather that he work for the mosque. Yes?

The old man stood before me, his eyes blinking into mine, a half-smile stuck above his beard. Then he suddenly let out a whoop of laughter. He put down the box and embraced me, and began to give thanks.

Without His will, not a leaf moves! When He wills it, man moves mountains.

Then he saw the tattoo on my arm and asked if that was my name. I nodded, and before I could stop myself, I found myself repeating a dialogue from one of my hero's old films.

People like us are born to move the heaviest mountains. We move them, we always have, for those who sit on peaks and think themselves the lord. Some day, maybe we will learn to move the mountain in such a way that when we let go of our burden, it is standing upside down and there is nobody sitting on top of our heads.

Soliloquy of the Unnamed Boy Found Face Down in the Ditch

This place is not the most beautiful place I have ever seen. It is not even the second most beautiful.

I want to go home.

Someone please call my uncle. Someone, please.

Delivers Another Rambling Lesson Forty Students Suppress Yawns

Whichever way you tell the story, memory should not become a millstone around your neck.

Yashika? You're bored? You must be wondering, why is Garuda sir always telling us these kings-and-war stories? Why do we have to read History? We want to learn Computer Science, maybe English. A little bit of Physics-Chemistry-Biology. You all want to be doctors, yes? Who wants to be a historian? Raise your hands.

As I thought. Oh? I see one hand.

Shiv? Good. But remember, history will lead you into more and more classrooms. Are you sure you want to end up like Garuda sir?

Ah! Archaeology. That's the sexy stuff. Digging up mummies. You see yourself digging for buried treasure? Indiana Jones, eh? It's okay. Indiana Jones is not as bad as, who's that other guy? The one who wakes up the mummy?

The things these Americans come up with. A curious mix of science, horror and fantasy. Waking up mummies. We do have a mummy in our country, did you know? A mummified lama. Ask your parents to take you to Spiti during the summer vacation.

Archaeologists go digging for Truth. Capital T, Truth. Evidence. Objects that give us the faint outlines of a story. This puzzle of the self. Who are we? What is the basis for our ideas?

Nobody can give you the whole truth in one easy-to-swallow capsule. No scientist, no historian. A man is many things—short and fat, bald and brave, sad and bad—simultaneously. You alone are aware of the fullness of your truths. Still. We need to gather the pieces of the puzzle, construct simple stories about our society. Like we tell stories to small children. '*Once upon a time, in a kingdom far away, there was a king, and he was brave and noble and much beloved...*'

So, the obvious question: why do some people in the kingdom—in every kingdom, in every era—want to bring down the noble king?

Annie Zaidi

Religion is never the motivation. Muslims brought down most Muslim rajas and nawabs. It should be obvious from what we have read so far. Hindu kings brought down Hindus, even before anyone had coined the word 'Hindu'. Buddhist, Jain, Sikh, all of them. The English and French were fighting each other. Spanish and Portuguese too. Centuries of colonialism, imperialism, slave trade—none of it was about Christianity versus the rest. It was about getting the better of your peers.

Deepika, you may now move to the back of the classroom. No, I don't want to hear an apology. Please take the last bench. From now on, you will not share your bench or your tiffin, at least not in my classes.

Luckily, the history period is before lunch. After lunch you are all supine. I, on the other hand, am greatly energized after lunch. The period immediately after lunch is my favourite. This is because I eat very light. Just a few dry nuts. Anyway, they are paying me peanuts, so what else should a man eat?

Fareeda, no need to blush. Teachers do not usually talk about being paid, but there is no rule that we cannot. You are told: teaching is a noble profession. As if payment was just an accident or a bonus. But as you know, teachers in ancient societies expected to be paid rather handsomely. Land grants. Cattle. We have a fantastic tradition of making extreme payments to our gurus. Pay by severing your thumb, if you are an archer. Pay by parting with your whole kingdom if you are a king. Pay the equivalent of the universe if you...

Anyway, I would love it if your parents paid me in land. Cattle? I am not so sure of. I don't have a wife who will clean the dung and milk the cows. I'm guessing it was guru-wives who got stuck with all that when their husbands were paid in cattle.

When a king acts in the name of God, or various gods, then it is useful for his opponents to counter him by aligning with a different faith. This causes a split in the public mind. Distancing yourself from existing power structures while simultaneously making a grab for power. These are old tricks. If it is not God, then it is skin colour. Two sides of the same coin: decision-making based on identity.

Our foreign rulers were mostly businessmen. They were bad business for us brownies. Millions died in famines. Slow, horrible deaths. Much worse than dying in battle. The landlords, the kings and princes who did not protect the poor against famines, they too are criminals of history.

Consider this: those who are eager to take credit for defeating a local ruler, should they not also be ashamed for having helped the white man create famines that killed so many poor brown fellows?

Annie Zaidi

Why did this happen? Did we look at white army officers and did our courage dry up? Or could it be that we actually did not care about the oppression of our own race? Everyone is constantly playing for territory. Animals too. Dogs, big cats et cetera will mark their territory. They must have taught you all this in Biology class.

They don't discuss urine and stink marking in Zoology? They should have told you. Dogs. Wolves. Cats. They fight with each other but there is no moral position. No argument about who invaded first, who is more aggressive. They just fight over territory. Territory and mating. But that's a lesson for Biology class.

In the human species, we need to justify wars over territory. In the name of God, or righteous conduct, or free trade. Kings, elected representatives, armies. Police. Imam. Pundit. Pope. It's like a chessboard. Who plays chess here?

Nobody plays chess? Please ask your parents to buy you a chessboard. It costs nothing. Your bat and ball games will not take you very far in life. Especially if you want to spend your lives sitting in air-conditioned offices.

I do hope that you will not grow up to become one of those idiots who hang a basketball ring inside the office. Ball in the basket, ball out of the basket. I say, what nonsense! Anyone can put a ball in a basket when he's alone in a small room and nobody is trying to snatch the ball away from him. The game is all about taking the ball away and scoring against a rival team.

Anyway. We will talk more about sports, symbolism and power grabbing in Civics. Where were we? We had finished reading about the Third Battle of—?

Who said Plassey? We're reading Plassey, Yashika? Where? In a parallel universe?

Oh, sorry. I forgot you were not present last week. Sick leave. Of course. And you, Fareeda? You were present last week. Remember?

Ah! Present, but absent. Well! Shiv, can you tell me where Plassey is?

Bengal, yes. It wasn't 'West' Bengal yet. Partition came later. Class 10-B, please note. Plassey is in the east and Panipat is in sort of the centre-west heart of the country. What kingdom was Panipat part of, at the time of the third battle?

Maratha, correct. Open your books to page 254. Yashika, will you please read out all three paragraphs on this page. And kindly read as if you have eaten some breakfast. Loud and clear.

Yashika's Soliloquy

I will remember him today. Each word he said, each time we met. And then I will forget.

The last time we met, he let me know that he was the better travelled one.

I have seen seven other places, before coming here.

I had tossed my head. So what? I have been to seven places too, I said. But the truth is, I have actually been to only five places apart from this little town. He didn't say anything, but smiled as if he knew something I didn't. It put me in a huff. I told him my father was going to take me to see ten new places this year. In the summer, we would be going to visit a foreign country. Europe, I said, knowing that he had no idea what Europe means. After

I clear the board exams, I'm going out of the country, I said.

He didn't say a word. His hands were busy, training the creepers up. I asked, so what was so great about these seven places that you have seen?

He shrugged. As if to say, nothing. The way he shrugged, with one shoulder, it was his special thing. I'd noticed it. When he didn't want to answer, he would give that one shoulder shrug.

That day, I would not let him be. I persisted. Is this not the most beautiful place of all the places you've seen? He paused in his work. He smiled, not looking at me, and inclined his head. It could have been a yes. It could have been a no. He did not say it, I thought that he must be thinking, yes, it is true. He just didn't want to admit it.

This is a summer destination, after all. So much good weather here, it's practically crawling out of my ears. People come here and blow up a lot of cash, just to stay a few days. And there is no estate house more beautiful than ours, stapled into the side of this gorgeous green hill. Vinny Uncle would say that it would make the tourists squeal with pleasure, just sitting here in a chair with one perfect, light cardigan knotted around their necks.

They pay just to sit and gawk, Timmy! I'm telling you. All they want is a simple bed and hot water in the taps.

Annie Zaidi

With your location, you'll get top-class crowd.

My father, nodding into his drink, saying uh-huh? After Vinny Uncle is gone, he and my mother always exchange their tight-lipped smile. It's their special smile. It means poor Vinny does not know the meaning of top-class crowd. They never say it, not in front of me. But when he sent for extra labourers, I asked if we too were going to have tourists. My father laughed.

Darling Yash, one cannot 'have' tourists. One can only serve them. The word 'guest' is a misnomer. If they're paying you, you're serving them.

My family is not inclined to serve anyone, not even itself. Darling Yash learned to make a cup of tea only because she had to pick a stall to work at, during the annual school fair. Amma got the cook to bake me a dozen sesame carrot cakes, but Fareeda ratted to the class teacher. I got a long lecture on how school was about doing jobs and learning and blah blah. Then she said, okay, you can sell the cake but you also have to make and sell tea. Fareeda had to teach me.

I told Majju that, talking to his back all the while. To his bare shoulder and his red vest. Fareeda has taught me to make tea.

He didn't turn. The pepper vine had his full attention. Fareeda, I went on, is my bestie.

Silence. Not a forbidding silence, though. A light,

feathery silence. Like butterflies. Do you know the meaning of bestie?

Another one shoulder shrug. Bestie means best friend, I said. Like the closest person, to whom you tell all your secrets. Do you have a best friend?

His shoulder moved again. His yes-no-maybe shrug. The butterfly of his silence was skipping around my head, distracting and soothing at the same time. I walked around to face him. He glanced up from his work but only for half a second.

Fareeda is from your community, I said. I tell her everything. I have never been to her house yet, because it is quite far from here. But after the exams, I will. She doesn't have parents, you know?

Majju's eyes darted around my face for a second. His fingers stayed busy. I lapsed into silence. His kind of silence. Watching him, but without looking at him. At last, he spoke.

Lots of us don't.

Well, at least she has a brother, I said. I don't have a brother or a sister.

I had one sister. She was buried without a name.

I asked, how come? But I kind of already knew. She must have died at birth, or just after she was born. His people are from the north, from the plains rather than the hills. A faraway village. He never told me the name of the village where he was born.

Our estate isn't big enough. If it was big enough, I would never have seen his face. If I did see him some day working with the vines, then he would not be anywhere close to the house the next day, filling water at the garden pump, or coming to the back of the house to eat his lunch. If he hadn't been close enough to the house, I would never have noticed that his eyes were light. Light eyes, like mine. His are brown, amber almost. Mine are green.

My Uncle Mommad says, never trust people with marble eyes.

Oh really? And what do you think you have? I had snapped, then I realized that although his face was serious and he kept his eyes lowered, he was teasing me. He was aware that he too had marble eyes. Little circlets of light. Stupid thing to compare them to, marbles. As if they were eyes of stone. I told him, we call them cat eyes. He looked up then and spelt out the word.

C-A-T, cat.

He never came too close to the house. His people live under tarpaulin tents on a strip of land just outside Vinny Uncle's estate. Once, when we drove past, I spotted him. He was squatting over a kerosene stove on the side of the road. Cooking.

Another time I spotted him while walking through

111

town with Deepika. We had stopped to eat a cream roll at Royal. And he was standing there. Not buying anything, just looking at the bakery goodies. He never said a word. I said nothing to show that I recognized him. But once we had walked past, Deepika nudged me and whispered about the colour of his eyes.

You know his name? I asked, knowing what she would say.

How would I know? We don't talk to them!

I told her, I know this face. He's one of the new labourers Vinny Uncle has sent over from his estate. I would have said more, but then Deepika let out a little whistle. She asked if he was staying on our estate too. The way she said it, I changed the subject at once, and began to talk about the trouble with our regular workers. They won't work longer than ten hours and they won't stay the night. But this lot, my father says, will do anything you ask.

Anything, except talking to you. Everything he told me, I had to prise out of him. If I said twenty sentences to him, he would say one. Strange things he said.

Yashika is not a very pretty name. But it suits you. It sounds like a foreign country.

I had laughed. Not a pretty name? I picked up pebbles and threw them near his feet. Not to hit him. Just to tell him that he was being silly. What a stupid thing to say! How can anyone's name sound like a foreign country?

Annie Zaidi

He would not explain. I picked up more pebbles and threw them at his shins. This time, I hit him. He took a step back. I threw more pebbles until I broke him down.

I had a school uniform once. Blue shorts, white shirt. I had a pencil too. I used to sharpen it with half of a razor blade. I had stolen that half of the blade from another girl. She used to sit next to me on the durree. We sat on a durree in school. Her name was something, I've forgotten it now. I broke her blade into two parts and kept half. I sharpened her pencil for her too. I used that half-blade to cut my nails too.

I never had a belt. I used a thin piece of rope when the button broke, to hold up my shorts. My mother's brother, Mommad, he had taken that piece of rope after untying the mouth of a sack. He used to load and unload sacks from trucks in those days. I never got to look inside the sacks. I really wanted to look inside. My uncle wouldn't let me go near the sacks when he got them off the trucks. But I know, there was rice inside.

Sacks cost a lot. We never got to keep the empty sacks. Here, we have to buy sacks to sleep on. They cost us more than a day's wage. My uncle says, one day we'll grow our own rice and our own pepper and our own cashew and our own coconuts. The world is a big place. If you walk long enough, you'll find a place that's not got anybody's name on it, and no fences around. There's got to be a place for us too.

113

Prelude to a Riot

I didn't stay in school after that first year. In the second year, they didn't give us new uniforms. The old shirt didn't fit me any more. I used to go to school with the shirt hanging open. The teacher said, don't come here like that. I told my father to buy me a new shirt. But there was no money. The year after that, it was too late. I never went back to school.

I wondered, how is it possible to live like that? To not even be able to write your own name! How can anyone survive without writing one's name down?

He held out his hands for inspection. They were full of cuts, but not ugly. Dark pink, un-fleshy palms. Neither big nor small. Long fingers. So many lines criss-crossing his palm.

I showed him my hands too. There are very few lines on my palms, I said, and he smiled.

That means nothing is written too deep in your fate.

That's when I asked. Do you want to see my school? I can take you, to see what it's like.

He neither said yes, nor no. Then I asked him if he had a full set of clean clothes. He never replied to my question.

I shouldn't have asked. How did it matter in the end whether his clothes were clean and not torn? By the time the watchman let us go, everything was made to look filthy.

Annie Zaidi

The Newspaper Does Its Job

'BOY FOUND IN DITCH, CAUSE OF DEATH UNCERTAIN'

A seventeen-year-old boy, later identified as Mujibuddin alias Majju, was found face down in a ditch yesterday morning. The body was discovered by passers-by who were on their way to work on a plantation in the vicinity, and who subsequently informed the police.

The spot where the boy was found is 120 kilometres from the estate where his family worked. He lived in a shanty on the roadside, along with several of his family members including his mother, two maternal uncles, two aunts, and five cousins.

According to his mother, Bina Rahman, the boy

had been missing for two nights. The family had not approached the police because they were not certain whether the boy had gone somewhere of his own volition. She said that although the whole family worked together on the same plantation, three weeks ago, her son and five other workers were sent to work on a neighbouring estate.

On Sunday morning, Mujibuddin was last seen wearing his only pair of trousers and a long-sleeved green and black checked shirt. At about nine o'clock, he told his mother that he was going into town. Ms Rahman assumed her son might be going to the cinema, or that he wanted to explore the market. She had not asked any questions, except whether he would return in time for the evening meal. He had assured her, she says, that he would be back before sundown. Mujibuddin appears not to have told any of the other boys about his plans for the day.

A citizen, who wishes to stay anonymous, told this newspaper that he was sitting in a bar, facing the road, and he did see a boy matching this description in the company of a teenaged girl, walking in the direction of Grace Higher Secondary School at about ten-thirty on Sunday morning. The watchman stationed at the gates of the school, however, could not confirm whether or not anyone had entered the school premises.

The official line of enquiry points to a hit-and-run accident. The post-mortem report is awaited and may offer some fresh insights. The investigating officer, T. G. Madhu, has said that it would be irresponsible to speculate further at this stage. However, police sources anonymously confirmed that other lines of investigation are being pursued.

This newspaper contacted several workers on both estates but they did not wish to comment on the boy's mysterious death. However, it must be recorded that when a local shopkeeper was approached for information, he spat on the ground and said, 'Just as well. Saved us a bullet.'

The owners of the estate where Mujibuddin worked, as well as the President of the Farmers Association remained unavailable for comment.

Tensions between workers, local as well as migrants, and farm owners, have been growing in the wake of rising material costs and labour rates on the one hand, and falling prices for agricultural produce on the other. This is, however, the first reported instance of a worker going missing or dying an unnatural death in this district.

Prelude to a Riot

Abu's Soliloquy

My grandfather has no vision. Eyes, yes. He has eyes for everything. Eighteen types of butterflies in our garden. Twelve types of flowers, four types of ferns which do not appear to flower, yet they do. I've never heard such lines in the mouth of a flesh and blood person. Bookish lines.

Flowering is human.

Flowering is human. Which is to say, flowering is everything that's alive. Which is to say, human is everything alive. That's my Dada. Can you win an argument with him?

Yesterday he came into my room. Six o'clock in the morning. Tapped my leg to see if I was awake. I hadn't slept all night. I wanted to keep my eyes shut but I knew it's pointless. There are things he sees with his eyes closed. God knows how, but he has always been able to tell whether our sleep is true or pretended.

It would be too much to look him in the face later, knowing that he knows that I had been pretending and trying to avoid talking to him. So I sat up. And what does he say?

Shhh.

I could have torn my hair out. Who comes into your room at six in the morning, wakes you up just to say, shhh?

I tried to listen. Crickets. A soft thup-thup. The dog was outside my window. Jumping up and scratching. I asked, so have you decided on a name?

You bought him. You should name him.

Didn't buy him. Didn't even find him. Devaki showed up with the puppy in a basket. Keep him, she said. For the estate. He'll be a guard dog. For Fareeda. She had cradled the puppy in her arms and kissed its neck before she tried to put him in my arms.

Don't, I had warned her. I'll just bring him back to your house and leave him tied up at the gate.

Okay. Then I'll bring him back to your house. Then, if you bring him back to mine, I'll bring him back to yours again.

Impossible. Impossible. A thousand kinds of

119

impossible. How to make her see? The heart of the world is not large enough. I should have taken the puppy outside town and left him at some bus stand. All the way back, my head was pounding with this thought. Let it die. Under wheels. Let it be taken by leopards. It'll be on her head, not on mine. Damn its whining. Damn it all.

I asked Dada if he had woken me up just to listen to the dog.

Listen. What do you think is happening outside?

I shrugged. He told me, smiling as if it was something to be proud of, that the dog had been catching butterflies in his mouth.

First, he tried for the big ones. The black ones, you know? With blue stripes on the lower wings? He nearly got one. Then he chased a black one with orange and black spots, almost like a colourful tail.

I would have said something unkind but he reached out to push open the window above my bed. Morning stepped into the room, cool fingers, damp wrists. Smelling of butterflies and dog.

He caught a little one at last. Snapped it between his jaws. One of the pink ones. You should have seen his face. He looked like he had caught a fireball in his mouth. The little thing must have flown about inside his mouth. He hacked, coughed, and out it flew. The butterfly, it moved like one of those drunken men in the market. And the look in your dog's eyes! He couldn't even bark, he was so stunned.

Dada sat on my bed, looking out of the window, quiet. I listened to him breathing. Perhaps he was listening to me breathing. I understood about the dog. He's no guard dog, just a play dog. Dada has turned my fearsome beast into a light phantasm, sheer as butterfly wings. A toy whining at my window.

Let him stay outside, okay? Not in the house. Should we call him Moti?

Instead of waiting for my answer, he shuffled out into the kitchen to look for leftovers. I knew he would make me breakfast too, now that he had woken me up.

Eyes and ears, yes, but no imagination. Moti. Pearl. Who calls a brown dog Pearl? He didn't do much better with our names. Abubaker and Fareeda. Picked out names without caring about meaning. My mother didn't care either. Let the elders choose, she said, and he picked any name he liked the sound of. Perhaps because someone with that name had a quality that appealed to him. Nice teeth or something.

What does Abubaker actually mean? I had asked once. He had no idea. He just thought it sounded dignified and scholarly. A name that would look good on school certificates. But he also knew that I was going to be called 'Abu' by anyone who knew me. Abu, short and sweet, the sort of name a first baby should have. One and a half syllables. That's all he wanted for me.

It was the same for Fareeda. He has no explanation for choosing her name. Must be a girl he liked when he was young. He'll never admit to it. Insists he just likes the sound of Fareeda. Two and a half syllables. Good for a second baby in the family, he says. He had decided on Fareed actually, in case a boy was born.

It annoys me when people refuse to look beyond the surface of things. Examine the meanings of words, I say. My sister does not sound or behave like a Fareeda. Not at all. She's a round ball of pertness, sarcasm and pigheadedness. Last summer I looked up her name on the Internet and told her the meaning. She was pleased to know, but the way she rolled her eyes!

Who cares what it means? My name is my name, that's all anyone needs to know.

There's sauce enough in that girl to set up a bottling plant. I gave her a thwack on her bum just to remind her who the older sibling was.

If I had a choice, I would have named her for an animal. Well, at least a wild flower. Something that grows in the forests. That would be in keeping with her nature. Or perhaps the banana flower. Red-blooded, thick-skinned. It doesn't have much of a reputation as flowers go, yet it is unique. A very practical flower. You can cook it, eat it. Full of flavour. A flavour that is neither

122

sweet nor spicy nor pungent. It is just its own thing.

Our bananas here are not the globby, half-sweet bananas they sell near the university. Our bananas have a sour undertaste, and a faint spicy scent. Maybe it is because we have spices growing right next to the plant. Something of one must get into the other. Like some of our pepper has got into Fareeda. She was born on the estate, after all. Right here, in the house, not at the hospital. Couldn't wait to be born, it seems.

Mariam says that even in the womb she was big and stompy. They were sure it would be another boy, the way she used to kick. That's why our grandfather had thought up a boy's name.

Mariam! She is also one number. She wasn't even around when our mother was expecting Fareeda. She came afterwards, when Dada needed someone to help with cooking and bathing the baby. But if you hear Mariam's stories, it's like she was here from the beginning. Before I was born, before my father married my mother. Sometimes, she even told us stories about our grandfather's boyhood, as if she had raised him too.

Pity I was old enough to remember when she first came here. Her blue and black saree. Her dark, flushed face. Hands clasped all the time, except when she was given the baby to hold. The breathy *haau! haau!* sounds she made while rocking the baby. If I didn't remember

123

it so clearly, then I could have asked about the time before, and I would have believed whatever story she chose to tell.

I want to remember with greater clarity the year before Fareeda was born. It is a big blank in my head. A hot, grey slate covered in chalk-dust. I see the faint outlines of a sketch, as if the chalk image has been wiped off carelessly. At the start of the year, I see myself in Amma's arms, cradled by her. She sings tunelessly. Her damp hair falls around my ears. At the end, Amma is on the floor, wrapped in a white sheet. There is baby Fareeda too, also wrapped in white cloth. Only, her face is visible. Amma's face is covered.

One thing I do remember. The sky was heavy with dark clouds. We had been waiting for the monsoon. For a long time, I used to believe that it was the same monsoon when my father lay on the floor, also covered by a white sheet. In my mind, it was the same day, and the same clouds looming in the sky. But it wasn't, of course. My father had died the year before.

The two images stand seven months apart. I used to check the dates again and again, to confirm and reconfirm the chronology but in my head, even now, these two images seem to be separated only by a day. One day, my father is on the floor and my mother is sitting in a chair, looking surprised. The next day, Amma is on the floor, wrapped in a similar white sheet. For a long time, I had even thought that the same bed sheet had been used for both events.

Next thing I remember is seeing my grandfather carrying Fareeda away. She is hidden in the folds of a white saree, slung across his back. I was supposed to be at school. My school bag was on my shoulders, a square hanky neatly pinned to my shirt pocket.

I remember hurrying behind Dada, the knot in my throat growing painful. I wanted to ask if the baby was dead too, but I couldn't form the words in my head. I followed at a safe distance, darting behind trees, wondering where he would bury her. But he didn't bury her. He went among the women who worked on the plantation. That's when I understood. He meant to carry her the way they carried their babies. Then Fareeda began to bawl.

That afternoon, I hid in the banana grove and finished the tiffin Mariam had packed for me. Upma, I still remember. The taste of fried mustard seeds, onions and the smell of banana flowers hasn't left me even now. For a long time afterwards, I used to confuse this date as being Fareeda's birthday, though of course, it couldn't be. Mariam started work here a month after she was born.

Dada used to say he carried Fareeda everywhere so that she would not miss her mother too much. I always thought it was wrong of him to think this way. How could the baby miss Amma when she didn't know her at all? Mariam says she was lucky to have got her first taste of mother's milk. But only for two days. I don't know if two days is long enough to know the difference between one's own mother and another woman.

I tried to tell Dada once. The baby doesn't miss Amma. He had drawn my head towards his own, pressed his lips to my forehead for a long time.

One does not always miss what one knows. Sometimes the thing you miss most is the thing you never had. But God willing, you will never lack for anything.

All summer I've been telling him about this thing. It is obvious to anyone who keeps their eyes and ears open. Right outside the white mosque, on three sides of Royal Bakery, they put up posters about the bandh. They didn't ask Kadir for permission. He might have said, yes, okay. But who asked him?

That's the thing, isn't it? To not have to ask. It means you don't have a right to say no.

Two hundred kilometres away, a bandh. The Self-Respect Forum is putting up posters here. A bandh to demand what? Five hundred men from five districts will gather. They'll come in lorries. Nobody will talk about what they are asking for. There are whispers. They will carry stones in the lorries and throw them at shopkeepers who refuse to down shutters. They will burn at least one state bus. Then they'll cry, success! Bandh success!

Why put up posters here when the bandh is two hundred kilometres away? Kadir is complaining. Still, he does not remove the posters. He shuffles. He crosses his hands over his belly. He does not name names. We know who gets Self-Respect Forum work done around here.

People put up posters anywhere they like. Not like in foreign countries. There, they will complain to the police if there is a poster on private property. Here, see, there is a government poster for family planning. Over there, Clean and Green campaign. What to do, eh? Nobody cares about personal property here.

Royal Bakery. Blessings Jewellery. Rahmat Fashion. Eyes down. Shuffling feet. Crossed arms. All postered up.

Usual politics. Eh?

Her eyes turn away from the face of that piece of dried-up vomit. Why is he coming? Devaki asks.

You saw?

How is one to answer her? Is it possible to avoid seeing?

They follow me. Those posters. That man's leery face. You noticed? They've lightened his skin with Photoshop.

I listen to her in silence. She says we should put up counter posters.

Let's! I'll make a poster listing these people's contributions to society. One big zero. I'll write: Why are criminal faces decorating our walls?

Prelude to a Riot

I don't reply with, yes, let's! She hangs her head. *Abu...* she starts to say. Then, *Abu...* She stops again. *Abu... Abu... Abu...* That's all. What are we going to do?

Dada is the worst of them all. Blind and deaf as only he can be.

Self-respect is a good thing to have. Painful, not to have it. Perhaps they don't have it.

If they came and plastered the walls of our house with their vomit, he still wouldn't get the message. He would just get the wall painted over and call them pranksters.

There are pranksters everywhere.

Or, *Too many workers from outside.*

Or, if the message was too cruel, too blunt, he would say, *Fathers need to put idle sons to work. These days, boys have too much free time.*

If I had not gone away to university, I wouldn't have known the term for his condition. Denial. It's a disease. This household is infected by denial. Dada, Fareeda, Mariam.

Mariam! She ought to know. She's in and out of their homes. She hears what's said. Or do they lower their voices? But surely, she can read it in their eyes. Feel it on her palms, in the tips of her fingers. She kneads their flesh. Can such things remain hidden when the clothes come off? Doesn't the venom rise from their skin like a hot stink?

When I tell her we should leave town, she looks at me with gooey eyes.

Ayya! Little Abu. You've grown so thin from the hostel food. Stay a few more days. Let me put some meat on you.

I cornered her last week. I asked, Mariam, can't you see it coming? She waved her hands in the air, as if she was batting away a housefly.

People say whatever comes to their mouth. Should we let poison enter our eyes and ears?

Fareeda. Stubborn mule. I showed her some of the messages on my college WhatsApp group.

Who wrote this? Nobody in our town writes things like this.

I thwacked her on the back of her head. What does she know about this town? How many people does she know outside her school? As far as she's concerned, her three stupid classmates comprise this town. She tossed her head, sniffed.

I too have 'sources'.

She talks of taking over the plantation. If it were not for the storm gathering, I'd have been whooping and hopping around the house. Yes! Come on then! You do that, I would say. I'm off the hook. Yahoo!

She could do it too. Even now, at fifteen, she can handle things better than me. Dada could relax, grow old in peace.

129

I remember when she had first learnt to sit up, before she learnt to walk, she had this way of leaning forward. Fists held out, as if she was asking to be pulled to her feet. She couldn't wait to start walking. And the way she screamed if I refused to pick her up. Fat, wobbly ankles. The way she grabbed my fingers when I held them out.

How to make them see? Images spin in my mind all day. Fareeda walking to the bus stand, alone. Fareeda alone in the house at night. Nobody around for five kilometres. Nobody home except our grandfather and now, this butterfly-eating puppy. Such an idiot. He won't bark. Not even at the new workers with their mustard-oil smells. The only time he barks is when he's happy, and that's when Fareeda returns from school.

I can't sleep at night for the silence. Sometimes I'm afraid that the dog will start barking at night and that will mean a stranger is around the house. Then what do I do? At other times I'm afraid that he will not bark at the strangers when they show up.

I talked to Dada about Fareeda. He will have to send her to Inter college anyway next year. I said, let me take her along. I can leave my hostel, rent a flat. We can live together. I'll hire someone to cook and clean. Dada can come and go as he likes. But no.

A big city is the devil with a million arms. Ten million arms. Let her be.

Annie Zaidi

Blind and deaf, that's what. I told him what they were saying about three mosques. He acted like he hadn't heard me. I said it again. This time, I noticed that he was stepping away from me. Then, half a second too late, I realized that my hand was on his chest. I was hearing a faint *dhupp* sound. Too late.

That I pushed him was not the worst of it. The worst of it was that he didn't hit me back. He didn't say that I have been ruined by the city, by that devil with a million arms. He didn't say that I was a burden and a blot, and what would my parents have said if they saw me now?

The worst of it was that he reached out and pulled my head down and pressed his lips to my forehead for a long moment.

Don't stay up too late. Sleep well.

When he left the room, he closed the door so softly I didn't hear the click.

ABC Writes Scathing Commentary Guised as a Poem

Small change is man
Piddly coin in the new market that even beggars squatting
  outside the temple reject
Iridescent green gaze—worth what?
Nothing!
Elfin ears, square chin, less than nothing!
Laughable, the price of his limbs
Except of course, kidneys and liver and
Skin for man is a harvest festival
Skin him alive and he's worth the price of his skin

*B*eneath the rafters of new market establishments, men
  scurry
*A*s if a man was owed life!
*S*cience makes progress every funding cycle
*T*hey'll be growing kidneys and retina in a petri dish next
*A*s if there will be any need of eyes or sex then
*R*egard these two lakh rupees as charity, not compensation
*D*isabuse yourself—the boy was no more than two hands,
  two legs, a mouth, a belly
*S*ell his memory and put the money into any bank that
  does not spit in your face.
@ABC

133

Mariam's Soliloquy

All of them want to know what my secret is. Every lady guest wants Mariam, only Mariam. Why? Common sense, I say. Strength! What other secret can there be? Not everyone has my strong fingers.

What people don't understand is this: strength is not one big sack that a woman can step into. It is not a rope of steel, or a pillar or a wooden beam that holds up the roof of the house. No. Strength is a rainbow. Seven colours, seven types of strength.

The number seven is very special. Seven steps around the fire mean a lifetime bond. They say that when you go to Hajj, you go around the Kaaba seven times. Seven heavens and seven gates of hell. Seven oceans. And our little Fareeda, she was telling me that there are seven wonders in the world. Seven old wonders, and seven new wonders. Our country has one of them. The Taj Mahal. Ah! Some day.

Kadir says he will take me some day. Not just to see one wonder, but to see all the wonders of the new world.

You, I, and the wind on our backs. Just you wait.

I wait. But Kadir forgets all his promises the day after he makes them. He hasn't even taken me to see the Cheraman Juma. We can go and come back in a day. Or we could spend the night and come back. But he does not take me anywhere. He cannot escape his wife for one night.

She's got her claws in, deep. You don't know her, Mariam. **135**
She's got eyes like a hawk and ears like an elephant.

Such things he says. He calls her a witch. Yet, he will not take one night away from her and give it to me. He will not get us bus tickets to go to the seaside. I even said, let me get the tickets. But no. Wait, he says. And I wait.

So much I've learnt from Abu, my little grown-up boy. Grown so wise. It was he who told me that Cheraman Juma is the oldest mosque in the country. It was made by our people when they first came on ships.

Our foreforeforefathers. They built a mosque here to affix themselves into this soil. Wise Abu. No faith takes deep root in a new piece of land, he says, if it is merely brought over from elsewhere. It has to be built, using the same soil. Using pieces of one's heart and blood. Using the strength of one's hands.

My hands are my wealth. People who are used to lifting things, say, buckets of water, their shoulders are strong. Those who walk up the hills, their legs are strong. Those who walk with piles of firewood on their heads, their necks and backs grow strong. And Mariam? Her fingers and her wrists are strong.

I owe it to the bakery after all. If my father hadn't sent me to work there for Kadir's father, I wouldn't have these hands. All afternoon, I would knead dough. Pat it, roll it. Make fine, flaky pastry. Sweet, rich hearts. Mounds of them, piles and piles of them. Jars full of them. They sold, my pastries, hand over hand. The whole town ate my strength, shat out my strength.

Just thinking of those years makes me want to throw up. I couldn't remember a time when my hands had not been covered in dough. From six in the morning to eleven, then again from three in the afternoon to six in the evening. And the heat, God have mercy!

I used to think that hell must be something like the baker's kitchen. I would sweat until my body felt like it was burning on the inside. My hands would be dry from handling so much flour, and so much washing up.

Annie Zaidi

My fingertips were raw from grating so much coconut. Mornings I was numb, evenings I was nauseous.

How I hated pastry! Bread, too. I couldn't get it down my throat. Only meat and rice tempted me. And cool fruits. Watermelon, cucumber, tomato. All those years, I couldn't eat a hot meal. I waited for my food to cool down before I could eat. And then, I could not eat at all. At last I told my father, enough! Kill me, but free me from this hell. I can't take it any more. The only place in town hotter than that kitchen is the actual oven. I'll die, I said. I'll die right there inside that bakery.

If I had known he would agree to me quitting the job so easily, I would have said it years ago. Six, seven, ten years, before I finally did. How long did I slave there? Ten years, according to my father. At least twelve, according to my count. Maybe even fourteen years. When I first went to knead dough in the bakery, I was a chit of a girl. I hadn't reached my full height. By the time I quit, I was illiterate and suddenly too old for the young men. Too old to be a poor bride at any rate.

I wonder now if I was pretty. There are no photos of me, except for one passport photo that was taken for the ration card. Everyone looks ugly in those photos.

I didn't think of my face in those years. Nobody saw me, locked away as I was inside that baking hell. No schoolboys turned their heads when I walked past.

I never went to school. How is a girl to know her own beauty if nobody looks at her?

Kadir says it now. Pretty. Prettier. Prettiest. Such a long tongue on that man.

I thank the angels for keeping you hidden away in that kitchen for twelve years. All hell would have broken loose if you had been outside and walking down the street, looking this pretty. The whole town would have got a crick in the neck.

My youth was gone by the time Kadir turned his head to look at me. Why did he look in the first place? He spins a long yarn of honeyed crumbs around me, but he never tells the truth. I ask sometimes, if only to tease him. I do not know if I can bear to hear the truth.

Twelve years of kneading flour. Then the desolation of seeing that nothing awaited me outside the baking hell. Nothing, nobody. I didn't know how to do anything except cook. If Abu and Fareeda's mother had not died, if their grandfather had not asked around for a sensible woman to take charge of the kitchen, I would have had to go back to work in one of the town's bakeries. And if I had to do that, I think I would have killed myself. Just in time, Dada summoned me to the estate. And what a sight! Old man with a newborn baby strapped to his chest. First time I'd seen such a thing.

Every day I offer thanks and on Thursdays, I light

incense at the mosque out of sheer gratitude, that my fate brought me to Dada's household. Look at me now. I have also fallen into the habit of calling him Dada. And why not? He has looked after me, and through me, my father. So in a way, he is my grandfather too. He is an angel. And see how life has tested him! One son, gone. Daughter-in-law, gone. Sorrow has softened his heart. Never asked me to bake after I told him that it makes me sick. Fifteen years, I have not had to touch an oven. And when others began to call me for massage work, he never reminded me that he still pays me for a full day's work.

Fareeda isn't the only baby that needs good hands. God gave you skill. Use it.

So much I owe him, and I should just leave that family for no reason? Bavna says it so easily, leave that job. But who gave me a job when I needed it? Dada! And what can Bavna offer me except money? Money is fine, but can I scold her children as if they were my own?

My hands did not recognize their true talent until I came to work in this home. Baby Fareeda needed to be bathed and massaged everyday. Haven't I been like a second mother to her? Now you can't even touch her hair. Not even when she has a headache. Stubborn child. Still, thanks to her, I discovered a gift that was waiting to be tapped. Right here, inside my skin, fused with my bones, was my fortune. It was such a relief, to know that I could earn my bread even after these children were grown up and didn't need me any longer.

My own father never understood. I used to worry, he might force me to give up massage work. He cannot believe how much these city ladies want to pay, just to be kneaded and pounded. Something must be wrong with the work, he thinks.

Do you truly prefer to knead the flesh of strangers? The bakery would take you back, if you wanted.

How can I explain to him? I prefer it, yes. Washing dishes and scrubbing floors would be better than baking. But even if I did want to bake again, now I cannot work at any bakery that is competition for Royal. At the same time, I cannot work in Royal's kitchen the way I used to. Like a slave. This thing between me and Kadir, which is nothing and everything, how to tell anyone about it?

I tell my father, the smell of baking puts me off. My father stares, unbelieving. The smell of baking is the thing he loves most. Baked bun smells. Coconut and sugar smells. Milk and sour cream smells. It was the smell that convinced him to send his little girl, his only child, to work in a bakery. For a poor child, what could be better than to be surrounded by the scent of heaven, and the chance to eat cakes and pastry, free of cost?

Nobody understands my revulsion. Devaki, when she

was a little girl, she used to slow down every time she walked past the bakery. She would stand there for long minutes, just breathing in the smells. I would be huddled in a corner, trying to stay as close to the door as possible. I had caught her eye a few times. On Sundays, she would come to the bakery with her mother.

Perhaps it was the sight of schoolchildren that gave me the courage to say, enough! Those girls out in the sunshine, in their balloon skirts, long socks and buckle shoes. Crying out with joy at the smell of a cake. Me, barefoot, covered in flour. Nauseated. I began to think, anything would be better. Death would be better.

I used to think of it constantly. Death by fire. Death by jumping into the lake. I used to wake up from dreams where I was always standing on the brink of death. I still remember one very vivid dream. Three times I have had the same dream.

I see a little house with blue painted doors and poky little squares left in the mud walls for windows. Once I saw the house bare, as if it had never been lived in. Not even a bed or a tin trunk to sit on. Just a floor of beaten clay, painted red and white, and a broom standing in one corner. As if the house was waiting for a woman to step in and start sweeping it clean.

The second time I saw the same house, full of new things. On the wall there was a shiny poster of a green valley, with snow on the mountains, and a blue lake, and a little child, holding on to a goat. There was a line of shirts hanging on a string, and a chair with a green cushion on its seat. A saree, so new it was stiff with starch, was hanging outside the window, left to dry after a wash.

The third time I had the dream, the house was on fire. I saw it from a distance, from the outside this time. The house was on the slope of a hillside, on one of the estates. In my dream, I knew the estate and the owner of the house. I dreamt that I was staring up at the house, at the orange glow. As I watched, it seemed as if the house was slowly growing in size. Or perhaps it was only the orange glow that was growing. I knew that the fire was big and would eat anything in its path. I was fretting. I asked aloud, will it come downhill? The fire will reach us, will it not? And in my dream, someone, a stranger I had never met, magically appeared beside me.

What if it does? Let it take this rotten old hut. Let it. Nothing can touch us.

Strange dream. I have never seen that little house with blue doors in real life. I do not recognize any such estate around here. Nor do I know that stranger.

In those days, I used to hear strange voices at night. Late at night, after dinner, when I was trying to sleep, I would hear voices outside the door. My father's whispers would be low, urgent. Then another voice, saying that it

142

would be very hard without a bit of gold.

One chain and one pair of earrings. There's the man who irons clothes at the end of lane.

Throw in a pair of bracelets and there's a chance of snagging a mechanic.

There's one man in the village, one and a half acres. His age is something to think about though.

The fellow whose age was something to think about had a twenty-two-year-old son. I was just about twenty-five. At night, lying in bed, I used to think, just let me step outside and look at the owner of this voice. I would tell this voice to fix me up with the son instead. Look at my hands, I wanted to say. These hands have fed a whole town. They feed me as well as my father. You think I have any use for old men?

But I didn't say a word. It isn't hands they look at when they choose girls. It is faces.

Kadir says, my face is a live ember. There's a reddish tint to my cheeks that never goes away. It is as if those years of heat in the bakery have baked me proper. Kadir says I remind him of a honey cake.

This very minute, I would go to him. But his wife! Thorn in my heart. Not satisfied with being his first. Who can take that away from her? I would only be a second. A poor second. Hateful woman. She says she will kill herself if he marries a second time.

I almost said it aloud, let her. She's no better than one of those puff pastries sitting in the bakery's counter. Only for display. Well past the date it could be eaten. What sort of wife is she if he can't touch her?

But I don't say a word to him. If he does not divorce her, then she must be some sort of wife to him. She is the mother of his son. And I? What can I promise?

All those years, I was hidden away in the kitchen behind the bakery, working for his father. What if Kadir had spotted me then? Before his son was born. Before he began to think of Royal as the centre of the universe. There was a chance then. He might have thought of marrying a poor girl. A slender girl of fifteen. A hardworking girl who would give him half a dozen children, and who could bake the best pastry in town.

What foolish thoughts. As if Kadir could ever have. His father was not unkind, but he was not a soft man either. The old man increased my pay only once in twelve years. He would have wanted gold. Ah, why blame him? Everyone is like that. Only Kadir is different.

Strange. All those years, he must have come into the kitchen sometimes. How is it that he never noticed me? Well, I must have been a wretched lump covered in flour and sweat. But how is it that I did not notice him?

We only noticed each other when I began to go to Royal as a customer, to buy cakes and biscuits for Abu and

Annie Zaidi

Fareeda. Good children, these two. They never asked for twenty items a day. Good, quiet children. Twice a week, I myself would go out and buy them treats. It was so new, the experience of buying instead of baking. I would stand and stare at the counter for long minutes. The assembled wholes, so different from how I remembered them. The neat, colourful squares, the crisp heart shapes. I would stare, trying to understand why people wanted to eat them.

Kadir would stare at me. Still. It took him years to say a word. To ask if I wanted to sample a chocolate bomb. A new thing. I didn't say I wanted it. He brought it out anyway, and put it in front of me. After that, every time I showed up at the shop, out came a chocolate bomb. Then, one day I saw him on the street. I was going to one of my massage jobs. I don't know where he was going but he stopped when he saw me. We just looked at each other for a moment. Then he turned around and began to walk towards the ruined temple. He turned, and looked at me. I don't know why, but I began to follow him. One turn, a look over his shoulder. That's all. No words. No promises.

I can hear the things Kadir will not say. This much I have learnt after years of working in people's houses, cooking, touching skin and hair, kneading hungry flesh. Listening to the things people can never bring to their lips.

Massage work has saved me from myself. All the things I could not tell anyone, all the tears I cannot shed because there is nobody to wipe them away. When I work at the knots in the shoulders of other women, I find some of my own knots melting.

What if I were just peeling potatoes, chopping fish, changing bed sheets? What a bore. It is my good luck that so many women from my neighbourhood called me to massage them after they had babies. That's how Bavna heard of me. These big city people had starting coming to her estate. They come for holidays. Walking, shopping, massage. There are ladies who have their own money, and their husbands don't ask why they spend so much. Bavna told me, just do it like you do it for little children. Three hundred rupees.

Three hundred rupees for half an hour's work? People throw money around like that? At first I thought Bavna was lying. She would quote one price, then the guests would bargain and beat me down. Ah! How little I know about this world. Three hundred rupees it was. And that's after Bavna kept half for herself. Then some of these ladies started asking for a full hour's massage. My ears burned just hearing the price. One thousand! Just to be touched and petted and oiled and kneaded like a lump of dough!

For a whole week, I fretted. What if my father was right? Perhaps there is something wrong with this line of work. Why else do people pay so much for it? But then Kadir set me right.

You are not like a barber oiling someone's hair. It is therapy. Like medicine. You have a gift from Allah. Does anyone think so much about money when one needs medicine? Don't they do it after new babies? For babies, for new mothers. For grandparents, aching legs and backs. You drive out the pain. You are a healer.

He showed me how doctors in white coats do it. These days everything can be learnt on video. And the moment I watched a few, the way their hands moved, I knew. I am made for this job! The strength of fingers and wrists, the sensitivity in my palms, knowing how much pressure to put, it was for this reason that Allah kept me slaving in that bakery for twelve years. I have come out of that furnace baked like a clay pot, to be used for the purpose of healing.

Now just look at this girl, Devaki. Two streams pouring down the sides of her face. This rain started the moment I started to rub her back. Half an hour now, and it hasn't stopped pouring. The real pain is not in the muscles but inside the heart. My hands unplug it, churn the vat of pain, let it run its course along the lines of blood, let it fall from the eyes. Doesn't this make me half a doctor? A nurse at least. And no school certificate, no college degree, nothing!

Not that anyone needs a college degree to make a woman cry. Kadir laughs when I tell him.

Only you women are like that. I never heard of a man weeping during a massage.

Hah! As if he has ever seen a man getting massaged. He has seen nothing outside this little town. School, then college, then Royal Bakery. His father did this, he does this too. He does nothing else, goes nowhere else. He doesn't even go to visit his wife's people. He packs her off when she wants to go, picks her up at the bus stop when she returns. Not that she goes anywhere these days. Pity. It would have been easier for us, now that the son is not living here.

Kadir says his wife doesn't go for long visits these days because her people don't have air-conditioning. Even fans won't work in that village because the electricity comes and goes, comes and goes. Fifteen times a day.

One year of air-conditioning. That's it! Suddenly she is a royal lady. She cannot sleep without cool air. That prince of hers has turned her into Queen Mother. Next time the electricity goes off, she will need slaves fanning her, right flank, left flank.

It is poor consolation that Kadir will not sleep in the room with the air-conditioner. He has been sleeping in the outer room on the divan. The more nonsense his son brings into that house, the more he shrinks into a tight corner.

Annie Zaidi

Unnecessary drama. Father wants son to study, become a big officer. Son refuses to sit for the civil services exam. Father says, don't think you'll inherit my bakery and sit behind a counter for the rest of your life. Son goes off to the Gulf. Brings back a microwave oven, air-conditioner. Father asks him to take it all back. Son says he wants his mother to live in comfort. Father says, this is my house. Son says, I'll take my mother away then.

If only! If only! I pray for it to happen night and day. Let the boy come and take his mother away. Let her do all the holy travels. All the shopping. All that timtam. Let her go, please! But can I say this to Kadir? He's all cut up. He can't stand his son's money.

If there is one thing you are not destined to get, it is the thing you long for the most. I should not have wanted it so badly. A son in government service! My desire is the stick with which Allah beats me.

So it is. And my desire is the stick that Allah beats me with.

I tell Kadir, let it go. The boy never had your ambitions. Every boy wants to go abroad. They talk to older boys, follow their example. He has a job, doesn't he?

Ah, but they work in petrol pumps! They work on construction sites! Labour class jobs. He is wasting his life. And for what purpose? He comes back with a bag of chocolates from the airport. What do we want with chocolates? His mother takes a day and a half to unwrap one of those thumb-sized packets. She makes such a noise with the wrapper. I get up and leave the house whenever I hear that crinkling sound.

He will not touch the chocolates. It is like swallowing the ashes of his dreams. Nor will he touch the money. Whatever his son sends, his wife puts into her own bank account.

I breathe easier, knowing she has money put away. I can live by the strength of my hands. Kadir need not feed me. The more his wife has, the better it is for us. But on the other hand, the more money her son sends, the sharper the blade of her tongue. Yesterday, they had bitter words. Kadir told her he could afford to feed two wives, should it come to that. She is free to go and keep house for her beloved son.

She just laughed. Wretched woman. His face was so small, like a mouse, when he came to cry on my shoulder.

This man is like a coconut. Rough on the outside, soft inside. If only his puffed-up son would stick to his word and take away his beloved mother. She can sit in the Gulf in air-conditioned rooms and her son can pour a bucket of chocolate over her head three times a day.

But she's not going anywhere. Abu has told me all about how these boys live in the Gulf. Squashed like worms, ten to a room. They send cash back so the fools at home can build cement houses and thump their chests like they're worth something now. Only one out of hundred men who go there can live decently. With their families. No respect over there, Abu says. Boss snaps a finger and you are out. Not just out of the job, but out of the country. And not just the labour class. Engineers, managers, anybody can be dismissed with the snap of a finger.

I say nothing to Abu but for people like me, it's always like that. Snap of a finger and out you go! Fareeda is grown up now. Dada still pays me, not just for the cooking and cleaning of the house but also for her care. But he could say, no need for your service now, please don't come from tomorrow. Then? Finished. It's the same, here or there. Only difference is, at least here you are not thrown out of the country.

Abu, bless him. So much knowledge in his head. History, politics, cinema, poetry. What can an illiterate woman say to such a boy? I often think of saying, have you seen your grandfather's waist? His back is starting to bend. It will bend a little more next year. Come back home.

I don't say it though. Only once, I said something. I saw him standing outside the white mosque, chatting with Kadir. I almost turned around. I don't like Kadir to see me and pretend that we are nothing to each other, so I avoid greeting him in public. But there was Abu, holding up his arms, shouting on the street.

Mariam! Oye, my Mother Mariam! Come here!

Mother Mariam. When he wants to tease me, he talks like that. There was laughter in his voice that day. I thought, good! It has been days since I heard that boy's laughter. He has been drooping around the house all summer.

Seeing his bright mood, I teased him back. I said, studying hard then? Is he your new schoolmaster?

Kadir's face darkened. At once, I realized my mistake. He doesn't like to be reminded of young men who are studying to become great, big officers. Abu is going to be some kind of officer. Or a teacher, at least. Better than being a loader or a welder in the Gulf.

Too late. The words were out of my mouth. I didn't dare meet Kadir's eyes. I simply nodded at both of them and would have rushed away. But those Self-Respect people appeared at the end of the lane just at that moment.

I had forgotten, it was the day of the Self-Respect march. All these people, dressed up in their fine clothes. They had taken out their weapons. Bavna's father-in-law was leading, a gleaming sword in his hand. Her husband Vinny was also there, with a rifle slung across his shoulder, carrying a poster in his hands.

Until last year, they would gather at Town Hall after

breakfast and march in a circle. Then some of the young ones went to the martyr's memorial to pose for photographs with their swords. It was the first time these Self-Respect people were marching straight through the heart of town, starting at Town Hall, past the white mosque, down to the bus stand, and ending at the martyr's memorial. First time they had a politician's face on the poster.

We stood there, our backs pressed against the walls of the mosque, until the crowd had walked past us. Then our Abu, what does he do? He jerks a thumb towards Vinny.

Don't you adore that fellow? Now there's a son who always obeys his father.

It made me uneasy, the way Abu said it. His mocking way. I said to him, these people also give me my bread. I will not say anything against them.

But do you like him? Is that what a good son looks like? Eh, Kadir? What do you think? At least, he is not a loader or petrol pump attendant.

Kadir spat in the dust, though he had nothing in his mouth to spit out. Still, Abu would not let it go.

Did you know a top politician's adopted daughter owns land around here. She is an outsider. But Vinny and company have never listed her land as 'alienated' property. Fifteen cabinet ministers have bought properties here. Twelve movie stars. Do you think Vinny & Co. will march to their estates as well?

I lost my temper then. What do I care, who owns what? I own nothing!

Oh! Mother Mariam, you own this whole town. You own our hearts. We are all in your hands. You know that.

I saw then that Abu knows about me and Kadir. My face grew hot and I started to walk away, but he put his arm around my shoulders and held me back.

Wait! Wait! Let the marchers finish their marching. Stand with us and bear mute witness.

A sob rose in my throat and I tried to push his arm away but Abu tightened his grip.

Do you know the meaning of outsider, Mother Mariam? An outsider is the person who can be kicked out easily. The one who cannot buy guns in the name of his tradition and caste. One who is not a minister in any government. Outsiders are 'out' of a charmed circle. Those who are within the circle of safety, they cannot be called outsiders. Yes or no?

Every time he said 'outsider', his lip curled. I shook his arm off and told him that he was a fool. A fool with big words.

You are too old to be wasting time, hanging around bakeries and tea stalls. How much tea-coffee will you drink? Help your Dada on the estate, I scolded. Why live off an old man's labour? And if you don't have the stomach for farming, then get a job. Go to the Gulf.

Go and be an outsider there. Work at a petrol pump.

Abu did not blush or cringe. He laughed.

Why would I go to the Gulf? I'm finishing my MPhil, then I will enter the civil services. Then I will take Dada and Fareeda and you, and we will go live in a fancy government bungalow.

I glanced sideways at Kadir and my heart shrivelled. I was afraid that he would start weeping in front of this foolish boy. I was about to scold him again but Kadir took a deep breath and patted Abu's shoulder. He struggled to lift his lips into a smile.

Civil service, eh? That is good. Very good! You prepare well for the exam. Your grandfather will be so proud when you become a big government officer. Not just him. All of us will be proud. I will pray for your success.

155

Later that night, Kadir came to my house. My father was fast asleep. I was lying awake in bed, prayer beads wrapped around my fingers. Sleep would not come. I went over the beads seven times before I heard the tap-tap at the window.

My hands are my gift. What else can I give? My hands on his back. My hands to undo his knots. My hands and his feet. Not one word passed between us, but hearts furling and unfurling within our chests. Streams running down temples. Mine and his, both.

Mariam, take me away from here. Let us go somewhere.

Prelude to a Riot

We will see the wonders of the world. That mosque you wanted to see?

I wiped my eyes, and I wiped his eyes too. I said, yes, we'll go. As soon as your son comes and takes away his mother, we'll go.

Kadir sighed deeply, and then he said something very strange.

I want to build us a small house. I can see it in my mind's eye. It will be just a one-room cottage, with a red oxide floor. And a bright blue door. A cottage near the edge of the forest. Far from all this. Just you and me. I dream of such a place, Mariam.

156

Garuda's Soliloquy

So! No school for Garuda.

Good. Garuda was just a slot in the timetable for them. Words, periods, one following the next. Garuda was a pain in the bum. They'll borrow notes from ex-students, mug up, pass exams. After the tenth grade exams are over, History-Geography-Civics is over. Nobody will study History.

Not very bright. Bright faces, yes. Black, brown, grey, green eyes. The eighth and ninth standard kids, I'll miss them more. I would have had them for another two years. They are more open. The tenth is already half out of my hands. Still. One final lecture would have been useful. I should have walked into the classroom and given them one lecture, then said, okay, I'm leaving.

Why? Because they're throwing me out.

Why? Because I'm a drunk. They found out that I drink here, on the school premises.

But you already know that. I drink. 10-A, 10-B, you know this. You can smell it, even though I don't come too close to you. I don't ask any of you to come up to my desk. In the lunch break, I eat roasted peanuts and glug the drink in my flask. Well, maybe you did not know this before. You know it now. It's just one drink at lunch. Properly mixed with cola. No drinking straight from the bottle. That's too vulgar.

Your fathers drink, don't they? In the afternoons, too. You, yours! I've seen him in bars. Yours too, Shiv. The school principal drinks. Not in the afternoon. Not when he's sitting in his car. Not like me. But he drinks enough.

It didn't need to end like this. They could have just said, please resign. I would have given one month's notice and left like other teachers leave. Normally.

Hah! Normal teachers. They told me a few times. *Please be normal in the classroom.*

Garuda sir is not like other teachers. Normal means what?

Telling students how to pass exams. That's normal. Don't tell them things that are not prescribed in the syllabus. That's normal. Don't make any connections between what they learn in History, Geography, Political Science. Don't tell them how to think about war. Teach them the composition of Parliament. Don't talk about how people have been getting into Parliament in recent years. Don't discuss criminality, or the malleability of the definition of criminal acts. Don't compare present-day municipality officers with urban management policies in the seventeenth century.

Children, look here. Garuda sir is going away. He is sitting in his car. His flask is still full of the drink he had mixed in the morning. He was asked to resign on the spot, no need to take today's classes. The board summoned him.

One month's salary will be credited into your account 159 *at the end of the month. The school management does not need to offer any reason whatsoever for terminating service, as mentioned in the contract. However, informally, we can tell you, it is on account of consuming alcohol on campus. Also, because you never finish the syllabus on time. For the last three years, you had to take extra classes for the senior sections on Saturday and Sunday, because you never finish the coursework before their mid-term exams. We are also aware that you have been smoking cigarettes in your car, which is parked on the school premises. This is not only against school rules, it is also illegal.*

The management is not dismissing you officially. We

are letting you go, so you have an option of looking for employment during this one month.

The school management is a benign body. It privileges the human over the merely academic.

Who knows if they can find a replacement teacher in the middle of a school year? Will he, or she, be as good as Garuda? Will your final exam certificate be a useless piece of paper that gives you nothing except a sense of entitlement, and a set of false beliefs about yourself and your nation?

The management cares about what people say. They care about the source of your joy—is it kosher joy? Who is cleaning, who is clean. Who is running, who can be made to run. Standard management practice. Human is not the same as humane.

Children! Would you not like to meet Garuda sir one last time? Give him a farewell party. Normal teachers get one.

He is sitting in his old car. Blue, like the sky. He is having his farewell party outdoors, at the school gates. He can offer you roasted peanuts. He could buy you cold drinks from the shop across the road.

Yashika, listen now. Do not turn against yourself. Your parents would have pulled you out from school if this wasn't your last term. They'll send you away to college soon. Good. Ask them to send you abroad. Fight for it.

Annie Zaidi

Brown-skin experiences in a white-skin land will be good for you. Sleep with five different races.

This is life advice from a fired teacher. No normal teacher will give you such advice. They'll write you letters of recommendation. Wait. I'll write you a letter of recommendation, if you want to go abroad to sleep with a boy from a different race. Black. Native American. You'll have to learn to call them Native Americans. Or maybe they'll send you to a girls' college. The ones that have barbed wire or glass shards embedded in the boundary wall, and very strict curfews.

You'll go to a posh college and no longer wear a uniform. You will wear colourful dresses. A new dress every day. Every two months, fashions change. Shoes, sandals, hair accessories. You're a fashionable girl, I can see that. Parents will send pocket money. But too quick, money slips out of your hands. Down the grassy, dew-kissed slope of money, you will slide. For your landing, you will choose a soft, heaping pile of money.

Dalliance with a plantation hand, a bad memory. Or maybe a nice memory after all. Like tasting wild honey in the forest. A boy who never went to school. Smooth brown limbs, busy hands, steady eyes. You wanted a taste, didn't you? Steadiness, strength. A boy who had nothing. You found a way to extract something even from him.

All of your class is doomed to be tourists in the bylanes

of love. You get off scot-free, boys and girls both. The sort of boys who are found in ditches, face down, they are different. The girls who believe it when someone says we'll run away and get married, and then they end up in brothels in big cities. Those are different girls.

Look at your Garuda sir now. He is drinking alone in his sky blue car, eating peanuts out of a dented aluminium tiffin box. Same box, all these years. You will see him drinking in bars from now on. That cheap bar, across the road from Royal Bakery? Many of you walk past that bar on your way back home.

I will come to the threshold of the bar when the school bell goes. When you walk past, I'll wave. I may have a glass of rum in my hand, which I will raise towards you. You will hurry past, faces flushed, pretending not to have seen me.

It will probably be all right. When you know something bad is bound to happen, your heart starts to build its fortifications. Maybe your hearts too will beat fast, seeing your fine teacher in the doorway of a cheap bar. White shirt turning yellow, not even tucked into his pants. No shoes. Open sandals. Cheap rubber soles. You will want to cry and then you will hate this man. You will hate me for not shuffling away quietly, trying to get hired in some other school with three good references backing my resume.

Annie Zaidi

You will also hate yourself for hating me. Or maybe not. Maybe it's a slow habit. This hating habit. It's been coming along nicely, though.

Last words, children. Modern history is incomplete. I am sorry for not completing the syllabus. I should have taught you backwards. Started with modern, gone back to medieval, and ancient history last. That is a more sensible approach. Now all of you have a dung heap inside your heads. This king, that king, battle number one, two, three. But you don't understand consequence. Real world consequence.

Why did the white man think he could colonize us?

Because we were not united? Bosh! They've been parroting this lie for a century.

Who is the 'us', this 'we' that was colonized? Who is the 'white man'? Has there been any moment in ancient or modern history when 'we' were united? Such questions are key to authentic nation building.

Listen. 'We' includes Ajatshatru and Bimbisara. Magadh and Kalinga. Asur and Aryan. Genocide is not new. Nor is it patriotic.

Who colonized the Asurs? How many colonizations of the same tribe have occurred over four thousand years? We can widen the scope of colonization further. Were Neanderthals colonized by Homo sapiens?

If the white man's imperial quest, which is recent

Prelude to a Riot

and well documented, was inherently racist, and if their racism was a big reason why coloured people began to revolt and seek independence, then can we not argue that there was racism extant in the colonizations of ancient India? Because we do have evidence of distinct racial threads even among non-white populations, and there is apparent hegemony along caste lines.

Turn to page 304, Modern History. It says, India was partitioned by the British. It mentions a two-nation theory. It mentions the Muslim League and the Congress as two major political players. Indian National Congress. A few paragraphs down, you will see a passing reference to the Hindu Mahasabha. On the facing page, you see a group photo of independent rulers. All princes, if you notice. No princesses. In that same chapter, you will see a picture of people—nameless, almost faceless, people—walking. Walking towards a place of safety. Going wherever they are told to go.

I am not here now to help you read between the lines. Please read out of syllabus. A syllabus is 'set' for you. You understand? It is 'set' by people whose job it is to limit your knowledge. I am against syllabuses.

India lived in its kingdoms, each one its own little nation. The people had no power to choose their rulers, no power to shape their destiny. In the provinces, in the colony that India used to be, most people did not have the vote. There were a few democratic experiments. The future pulled us in two different directions.

No, wait. Let me correct myself. It pulled in four or five different directions.

Imagine the nation as a giant tent. A big piece of fabric woven with all kinds of fibre. Hemp. Cotton. Jute. Each strand had a different quality, but the thing held. It is a solid weave.

We progressed because we were mostly pulling together in one direction. Other forces were exerting an opposite pull, but most of us abhorred violence. What happens when a piece of cloth is pulled apart with some violence?

Force, motion, atoms. The fabric of the nation is made up of trillions of billions of millions of molecules. With strong forces pulling in opposite directions, the fabric rips. Atom is separated from atom. That's how it happens, children. At an atomic level. One by one, you are rent asunder. One by one, you are taught to pull in the direction of violence. But before that can happen, you must be rent within yourselves. You cannot easily be separated from your neighbour, your classmate, unless your heart has been separated from the pulsing of your own blood, your eye has been separated from your vision. Within your own body, you will find the germs of sundering.

No big colonial sword needs to come down and slash the fabric of the nation. Muscle by muscle, atom by atom, we are being torn from within. We are our own bomb.

Annie Zaidi

Kadir's Soliloquy

One thing you are destined to never get. This is the thing you crave.

Perhaps you want it so desperately that it starts to infect you, like a disease. Perhaps you want it for unsavoury reasons. I should not have wanted it—an officer son. A district magistrate. At least a police officer. A son who would be able to command the sons of my neighbours.

That boy has not one shred of ambition. Getting away, that's all he wanted. And those damned foreign chocolates. I have told his mother. You go and sit in that desert and let your son pour a bucket of chocolate over your head thrice a day. Wretched woman, she snorted.

And where will you go? Do you have another son tucked away somewhere?

I said, no. But I could. Even now. I could. Brazen woman. She said I spoke as if he were not my own blood.

Do you doubt that he is your son?

I warned her. Don't plant a doubt in my head, else you'll see.

Else what? She does not ask. I dare not tell. Else Mariam? No. Mariam is no threat. She is something else. A jagged missing piece of me. All those years, right here, behind this wall, crouched over mounds of pastry dough. Morning to afternoon. Escaping for two hours in the middle of the day, rushing to her little two-room house to make lunch for her father. All those years, never once did our eyes meet.

I worked in the bakery too, in the summer months. My father made me, and I did not protest. What was there to protest? I was learning more commerce here than in college. I must have poked my head into the kitchen once a day to take stock. Five, six, maybe seven years, she was right here, and we did not look into each other's eyes. How is it possible? Fathers, she says.

Your father managed the till, and my father took my salary from him directly. I never entered the shop through the front door. Directly, I went around to the back into the kitchen and waited for the men to fire up the oven.

Annie Zaidi

I would have shown up two hours after her. In the evenings, when I went around to the back to lock up, Mariam would have left.

Ah! His will. After my marriage, after my son was born, after my father's death, after I stopped wanting anything more, she came into my life. Her face, like a faded dream. Making me restless with recognition. Her eyes, searching for something that wasn't in the display counter. Time, she says.

Time had not touched the bakery. Tables, chairs, cups, plates, everything was like before. Only you were changing. And I was too.

Grey-haired Mariam. Drawing slant glances. At this age, prancing around. I know what is said. What to do? Allah gives what He chooses, at a time of His choosing. I did not know I lacked anything until Mariam walked in and stood puzzling over the cakes. I felt a foolish urge to follow her home, wherever she lived, to make friends with her husband or father or children, whoever held her loyalty. To ask for a little slice of her time. The right to look at her face.

I had not intended to jump into anything. That first time, when I was returning from the mosque and saw her under the open sky with the sun dancing upon her hair, turning silver strands into gold, and the wind pressed the clothes into her shape, I had only wanted to tell her how she appeared. Like a vision. Like an angel.

It struck me then that we think of angels as young. As young men, mostly. Or ageless women with smooth skin and long hair. Angels are those who are innocent, unmarked by life. At our age, nobody would think of us as angelic. But then, man is a fallen angel. Therefore woman must be too.

Mariam, patient with my cowardice. Patient beyond endurance. I cannot leave my wife. I married her when she was just fifteen. I cannot turn her out. She will not leave. And now that boy, Abu, he tells me to start packing.

You could still get a good price. Royal is in the heart of town. Do it while you still can.

Forces of history are at work, he says. Forces too big to fight. He reels off dates. 1947, 1857, 1799. I slapped my head. Spare me. I don't understand kings and queens. I am a simple man.

Simply put, Kadir, the writing is on the wall. My wall. Your wall. Rahmat's wall.

Slathered on the walls, wrapping all the way around the street. Every shutter, all the way up to the white mosque. It is true. That puffed-up face, like mouldy pastry. The fellow has called us aliens in our own land. He lost the election and we thought, that would teach him. Now here he was, his face pasted on my wall.

It felt as though the greenish glue used to paste those

170

Annie Zaidi

Self-Respect posters was squeezed straight into my mouth and nose, all the way up into my air passage.

Have you noticed any posters on their estate walls?

I crossed my arms and said, don't be a goat. Who puts up posters like this at home? But it was true. The boundary walls of most of their estates are pristine. Until last year, the Forum was content with plastering Town Hall. Something in the air is heavy this time. A feeling, like one should not step out of the house without an umbrella.

Saturday night, it rained. I closed the bakery and went into the bar. Garuda was there. He'd been at it all day. Kept saying there was no school tomorrow.

Freedom! Eh, Kadir? Freedom's a good thing to have, no? You would think so. What a man will not do to be free! But. Yet. Even though. Despite. But. Yet... 171

Mumbling. Not waiting for me to answer. Sometimes the men from other tables would cock an ear, and come over to listen to him for a minute. Then they'd leave. I must have sat for an hour, listening to the beat of the rain and Garuda's words washing over me like a light toddy. Then Vinny came in. Straightaway he dragged up a chair and he thumped my shoulder.

Business is good, eh?

Never before had I seen myself like that. There were mirrors on either side of the bar. I could see myself as if I was seated on the chair opposite. My mouth looked weak and sloppy, attempting to settle into a smile. My hands, too small, like a child's. Inept.

Lucky you! Sitting and relaxing, eh? I have not had any time to sit down. The rally's going to be much bigger this year.

The question of his posters on my bakery walls flickered, licked the corners of my tongue. I downed my drink quickly. I wanted to leave but I could not leave at once, not without offending Vinny. I nodded. He thumped my shoulder again.

This time, Kadir, you must help out. Shouldn't you be involved with our struggles? Otherwise, it gets difficult.

I did not want another drink but I raised a hand. The waiter came up and I saw myself gesture at Vinny. He gestured his usual at the waiter, then stretched and arched his back, then slapped my shoulder again. This time, he did not take his hand off my shoulder.

Someone puts up people in their hotels. Someone gives money. So many things to take care of. You must show your support. Meals free at Royal. How about that?

It must have been written on my face. Garuda saw it. He put his hand out, right in front of Vinny's face. Brother, we have met, he said.

Perhaps at a parent-teacher meeting. I know half this town. Well, the moneyed half. But I'm done with all that. I guess we'll be seeing more of each other now. The bar is set quite low. Huh? Haha! Now tell me about this rally.

Annie Zaidi

What is the cause? But first, tell me your name.

Garuda slapped a hand on Vinny's shoulder and he did not remove it, not until the hand weighing down my shoulder was lifted. It was like a thick fog had been pierced with a thin needle. The smallest glint of silver reached me. Still, so cold. I shivered all night. The next day, my lips arranged themselves around the words: Sell it. But who would I sell to?

I sensed that Mariam was willing herself to be still, to collect herself before any words escaped her.

You will never sell. Royal was started by your grandfather.

What does it matter? I said, there's nobody to take it on after me.

Your son will return. Eventually, they all come home.

He might. But who knows if this will still be home. Will it be the home he left?

Abu's fretting is rubbing off on you.

I know she was waiting for me to contradict her. I didn't.

That greenish glue was filling up my mouth again. I retched. Nothing came up. The glue of those posters was sitting on my tongue, sliding down my throat. I went to the bar and drank the hardest drink. Turned my belly inside out. But they're still there. Green gobs of glue, like some demon's spit, stuck to the wall. All my walls. The walls of my stomach, my lungs.

Last night, after a long time, I had the old dream from my childhood. The beast and the infant. It is from that ruins of the old temple where Mariam and I go walking. The western face is wind-ravaged and you can no longer tell the difference between gods and devotees. The snouts of animals and the breasts of women have been blunted. But on the southern wall, there are strange beasts. Lions, or perhaps lionesses, for they have breasts, with the tail of a serpent and a little tusk on either side of their mouths. They crouch over the body of an infant. A row of twelve beasts, twelve infants.

When I was a child, I used to have dreams about it. The beast showing its sharp teeth, dripping thick threads of spit upon the baby's face. My father once took me to the mosque and asked a travelling fakir to sweep the bad dreams out of my head. The old man brushed my face with a clump of peacock feathers, but first, he asked me to describe the dream. Then he explained the meaning of it. The lion, he said, was courage. The snake was patience. The elephant was wisdom and memory. The infant was love. Guard it, he said, with your life.

Everything must serve the infant. Life is nothing without love and faith. Guard the most helpless thing inside you, with everything you have. Do not let the beasts of memory trample it. And do not keep your heart hungry for too long, or it will end up eating itself.

Annie Zaidi

After forty-five years, I had the dream again. Only this time, it was clear that the beast was not guarding the infant. The lion's maw was wide open, as if it were about to pick up the baby between its teeth. The face of the baby was covered in slime and, in my dream, I knew that the beast's spit was venomous. One way or another, the baby was done for.

Today I said to Mariam, what if we went to the Gulf? Like my son. Not to live with him. Just to go away. I could work in bakeries there. Or do accounts for some shop. Ha! I bet that would make him come running back home. Don't you think?

The light in her eyes dimmed. She went into her kitchen to burn a fistful of red chillies and then waved it all around me. The smoke seemed to come straight from the fires of hell.

See? Somebody had cast the evil eye upon you.

Somebody must have, I said, but what to do?

Give to the new mosque fund. And at the bakery, pick out seven people and let them eat free. Do it for seven days. Seek their blessings. Draw the good towards you.

I did not say to her that goodness cannot be seduced, that blessings don't come with bribes. I drew her close and breathed in her smell. Coconut. I kissed her fingers, smelling of onion, and something sharper. Salty, metallic. Iron.

Prelude to a Riot

Dada's Soliloquy

A fuller moon than any that has ever been seen before in my stretch of sky. Blood-speckled. It is a true name, after all. Blood moon. I have lost.

When Fareeda came home from school yesterday, she said that her History-Geography-Civics sir had asked all students to sit out on the terrace between ten and twelve at night, and look out for the blood moon. I had frowned. In my heart, I cursed this History-Geography-Civics teacher. Why put a curse upon the moon? The moon is a dear, darling thing. There is no blood on it.

I told Fareeda there is no such thing. I could not bring myself to even repeat the words, blood moon.

Well, I'm going to see it, she huffed. I could not let

her sit out on the terrace alone at night. But no, why malinger in half-truths? The truth is, I wanted to see it too. I said, I can bet you anything—a big bar of coffee-flavoured chocolate—there is no such thing. But now I have seen it, the moon's golden face tinged with blood.

Gold-red moonshine brushing her face. Little baby, even now. Little, little girl. The same round eyes from when she was five years old. Her round glasses make her look like a small animal. No vanity yet. She is so far from womanhood, she is scornful even of kajal.

The moon showed itself a half hour after midnight. Abu tugged at my arm to rouse me, and there it was. Low-hanging, as if it had to come a few steps down on the ladder of night. For our sake. To reward the vigil of children and old men. Or perhaps, it was that the moon wanted to get a closer look at our faces. Fareeda's innocent face. Abu's handsome, worrying face, though tonight it had been coaxed into sweetness again. And mine, the colour of clay, lined as a furrowed field.

The moon looked at us deep and long. It looked between the gaps in my teeth, found the black thread of doubt ravelled into my throat and pulled it out, clean. I was free.

What a glorious dawn! All night we were up on the terrace, my two precious ones and myself, wrapped in a quilt made out of their mother's old sarees. The sky was like an oven slowly warming to the first bread of the day. The night sky, a lump of burning coal, now gold, and now fiery red.

By the time we came down from the terrace, the quilt was damp with dew. Both grandchildren were wide awake. It was such a precious night that I led them out on a little walk. First, we walked around the house and I pointed out once again all the different flowering plants—which ones their mother had planted and which ones my own wife had planted. We walked further, to the edge of the plantation. This piece of land that my father bought and cleared with his own hands, and which I have sown and watered with my sweat.

The dog was with us, his breathing loud. It gives me peace to hear that happy dog. My poor boy, his mind is soaked in fear. Last night, when we were up on the terrace and Fareeda had fallen asleep for a few moments, he started talking again about what is coming.

It may seem like it is light years away, but this sort of thing, it travels at the speed of light. It will be here one night, at our gates. And then? You think we can save anything? Not even this little dog.

I asked, what are light years? He buried his face in his hands. I asked him again. I said I am an ignorant man. I did not go to college like you and whatever little I learnt in school, I have now forgotten. All I know is the land and its riches. Pepper, bananas, coffee, rice. This is what I understand. Now, what are light years?

So he told me. I tilted my head back and looked up into the night. Tinsels of light, as long as the gaze could go. And yet, it is a ball of fire, isn't it? Not tinsel. I asked Abu, so every star is a big ball of fire?

It is. And when a large ball of fire is heading in your direction, you'd be a fool to not start running.

My boy. My boy's boy. So little when I first held him in my hands and whispered his given name into his ears. He calls me a fool.

Tonight, I went to his father's bookshelves. How many hundreds of trips my boy had made into the city, looking for new books written by people I have never heard of. Books about places I did not know existed. Peru. Botswana. Cuba. There was so much time after he left us. Screaming lengths of time. I had more free time than any father should have. One by one, I picked up each of those yellowing books. Poems. Romances. Stories of battles fought and lost. Of gods and goddesses. Ghosts and witches. These last fifteen years, I tried to read everything that my son had read in his short life.

I found the book I was looking for. My son had a habit of underlining the lines that struck him in a special way. I opened the book to the page I was looking for, and took it to Abu's room. He was lying in bed, awake.

I told him, this book belonged to your father. He bought it when he was in college. Then I pointed to the lines underlined three times in red ink.

Who could I hurt without damning my soul?
Who in this world is not my own?

Abu did not look at me but I saw that his eyes had filled. He turned his face away and mumbled.

Those people are blockheads. They have two sores for eyes.
They read nothing. They refuse to see your truth.

I left him and went to my own room. Sleep was impossible but I lay down and listened to the hum of dawn spreading her wings across the estate. I heard crickets, after a while even the crickets fell silent. I heard the dog wake up, scuff the mud, then settle down again. I thought I heard the moon rustle across the sky. A full, bloody moon. Red and gold. A bride's colours.

As I lay in bed, waiting for the morning's tasks, my mind's eye filled with the memory of the old white mosque. I saw little children, their steps quickening as they smelt fresh baking, turning the corner to rush towards Royal Bakery. A girl in a blue frock, a little amulet around her neck, the thread as black as her eyes. She is the heir to this place, yet to be born.

I saw an old man in a white cap, walking with his hands clasped behind his back. That must be me, my shoulders beginning to droop. I saw another girl in a black burqa, her eyes familiar and yet she is not known to me. Not my mother, nor my wife, nor my daughter-in-law. Who is she? Perhaps Abu's future wife.

At the mosque, I saw a kitten crouched upon a high ledge, staring at me out of startled amber eyes. If she fell now, she would not land on her feet.

I saw my garden, and a bunch of ripening bananas, the fruit only as big as my forefinger. Almost ready.

Then I heard the azaan from the new mosque. Then birdsong. Then it was time to get up and go.

Acknowledgements

I owe a special debt of gratitude to Sangam House, a rare writing residency in India that has consistently supported the production of literary works across genre. Through Sangam, I went to the Jayanti Residency offered by Pushpesh Pant at the Royal Mountain Hotel near Ranikhet. This little novel was finished there. Arshia, DW, Rahul, and Pushpesh, you are serious enablers who make the world better, and more bearable for fellow writers.

Musharraf Ali Farooqi was an early reader of this text, before it was a proper novel. I thank him for his feedback and support, and for his generous friendship.

I have been lucky to have a careful, considerate and enthusiastic editor in Simar Puneet. I am also grateful to

Thomas Colchie (of The Colchie Agency), and to David Davidar, Bena Sareen and the team at Aleph.

As usual, I must thank my mother Yasmin Zaidi, for all her love, support and tolerance.

184

Annie Zaidi